NELSON PAIGE
AND THE DREAM CATCHER

BARBARA J. LAMBERTI

KS
Kravitz & Sons

Kravitz and Sons LLC
204 E Arlington Blvd. Suite B
Greenville, NC 27858

© 2025 Barbara J Lamberti. All rights reserved.

No part of this book may be reproduced, stored in a retrieval system, or transmitted by any means without the written permission of the author.

Published by Kravitz and Sons LLC.

ISBN: 979-8-89639-541-6 (sc)
ISBN: 979-8-89639-542-3 (e)

Library of Congress Control Number: In Progress

Because of the dynamic nature of the Internet, any web addresses or links contained in this book may have changed since publication and may no longer be valid. The views expressed in this work are solely those of the author and do not necessarily reflect the views of the publisher, and the publisher hereby disclaims any responsibility for them.

TABLE OF CONTENTS

Chapter 1 : What If? 1
Chapter 2 : The BMX Wonder Boys 8
Chapter 3 : The Rebel Chief 15
Chapter 4 : "One Fish! Two Fish! Red Fish! Go Fish!" 21
Chapter 5 : Surprise! Surprise! 26
Chapter 6 : Advanced Fortunes 31
Chapter 7 : Indoor Treasure Hunt 34
Chapter 8 : The Dream Catcher 40
Chapter 9 : The Sweat Lodge 45
Chapter 10 : Chicken Soup 53
Chapter 11 : Vision Quest 61
Chapter 12 : The Maelstrom 65
Chapter 13 : May the Wind Always Be At Your Back 70
Chapter 14 : Connected to Nature 77
Chapter 15 : Rough It 81
Chapter 16 : Telegraphing 84
Chapter 17 : Let's Go Hunting! 87
Chapter 18 : The Waterspout 90
Chapter 19 : A Buffalo Mousetrap 95
Chapter 20 : The Buffalo Caller 101
Chapter 21 : The Prairie Eats Up the People 105
Chapter 22 : Cup-caking 113
Chapter 23 : Off and Running 117
Chapter 24 : The Treasure Chest 124
Chapter 25 : Wings of the Wind 128
Chapter 26 : Tinkling Bell 131

Chapter 27 : The Wings of Time 138
Chapter 28 : The Buffalo Robe 143
Chapter 29 : Pemmican 146
Chapter 30 : Parfleches 148
Chapter 31 : Girl Free From Evil Spirits 150
Chapter 32 : Familiar Shores 156
Author's Note 161

What others are saying about…
Nelson Paige and the Dream Catcher

"This would be a great book to use while teaching about the Plains Indians. Students learn about the life and origins of the Plains people as well as the animals and their importance in surviving. The carefully chosen vocabulary will help children paint a picture of what's happening in the story. This is a great book for 4-6th grade."
Melissa McCain, 4-6th grade teacher @ Papillion La Vista Schools, Papillion, NE

"The choice of words that the author uses really helped me paint a clear picture of events. It makes me want to keep reading to see what happens next. It also helped that I read *Nelson Paige and the Treasure Trove*, the first book in the series."
Jake 11, Grade 6 @ Walnut Creek Elementary, Papillion, Nebraska

"My mom read the book out loud to me, and I couldn't wait for her to keep reading. I learned a lot about how the Plains Indians lived-I can't imagine living like that! We've mad dream catchers in school. Maybe I should sleep with it under my pillow!"
Joey 8, Grade 3 @ Walnut Creek Elementary, Papillion, Nebraska

"Good book filled with lots of adventure. This is a book you don't want to put down. You will learn about rough living conditions of the Plains Indians long ago. The descriptions are so clear that you don't need pictures to show what's happening. You can paint your own!"
Nik Stevenson 13, Grade 7 @ Papillion Junior High School, Papillion, Nebraska

"Nelson Paige would be fun to be with. He likes the outdoors. I would like to go camping with him. Besides he likes Dream Catchers."
Michael Barbato, Discovery Canyon Elementary, Colorado Springs, Colorado

Dear Reader,

You are about to embark upon reading *Nelson Paige and the Dream Catcher*. The magic of Nelson's dream catcher takes Nelson Paige to meet Rides-Away-Tinkling, Elk-Woman, Buffalo-Calf, and Many-Painted Ponies of the Plains People. Through their eyes he learns about another culture's variety of customs, beliefs and values. It is a narrative that examines traditional family life, warfare and the ways environment shaped their lives rather than a culture lost in unfortunate images of being savages, alcoholics and communing with nature.

Nelson Paige and the Dream Catcher is the second in a series of four historical novels: People of the Forest and Lakes (Iroquois), People of the Plains(Pawnee/Cherokee), People of the Rivers and the Sea (Okonogan), and People of the Deserts and Mesas (Navajos).

In the first book of the series, **Nelson Paige and the Treasure Trove**, Nelson Paige visits the Treasure Trove antique store with his grandfather where he is transported into another time, space, and proportion as he discovers the magic of paddling a canoe. With each dip of the paddle, he is mesmerized and taken to a place of mystery and intrigue where he meets Wolverine, Beaver-Tail, Flying Chipmunk, and Buffalo-Heart. With each step he takes the life of the Native Americans is revealed.

In both books the narrative is told through the eyes of Nelson Paige—conversations, personal thoughts, day-to-day routines—to make it more readable. This is in no way to diminish the facts about the cultures therein, but a better way to appreciate and understand them as a people and to show the importance culture plays in developing self-image. There are varying kinds of information in the book. The time travel is fictional, but the information about the cultures is factual and based on my own library research. Quotes and anything borrowed directly from published material was placed into italics. It has been an interesting book to write and, I hope, to read.

BJ Lamberti

To those who dream dreams and travel
the distance to make them
become a reality.

"Dreams are journeys that take one far from familiar shores to unfamiliar shores where they strengthen the heart, enliven the mind, and empower the soul."

CHAPTER 1

What If?

Nelson Paige, in comparison to most boys his age, seemed normal on the exterior; however, his imagination and ability to dream would take him much farther than peers his age. One could tell at his very young age of twelve he was a person capable of dreaming and wasn't going to be one of those people who in the distant future would go to his death hypothesizing, ***What If?*** Nelson kept putting his imagination to the training stable—even though it meant stumbling, falling, picking himself up again and again, and then possibly not making the grade. He knew that anyone with a dream must learn to confront it sooner or later. Little did he know this meant delving deep inside and letting the light grow and grow and grow until it became as big as life itself. Only then was it no longer a dream but reality. Now the difficult part was finding a balance between dreaming and reality.

It was eight o'clock in the morning, and evidenced by his bedroom, Nelson Paige awoke from a most restless night of sleep after his trip home from the Treasure Trove with his grandfather. In the grasp of his hand was a dream catcher, a tiny souvenir purchased by his grandfather from the Treasure Trove on their recent visit.

"Ouch!" he shrieked with pain no less than three times.

Nelson had hit his cut finger against his newly acquired treasure. Have you ever had a finger with a cut—a cut only deep enough to make it start making you edgy to the point it made your stomach start turning? Well, Nelson Paige had just this, a superficial cut; nevertheless, it was uncomfortable. Carefully, he felt his finger, and the smart of the cut removed abruptly the tiredness from his eyes and put furrows in his forehead. Rotating his cut finger making sure not to make contact again with his unscathed hand, he tried putting things in their perspective as he remembered the ceremony that he had with his blood brother, Beaver-Tail. Surprisingly, it had a momentary quieting effect on his incision until a tickling, soft sensation was felt from a drop of blood falling on his unscathed hand. The simplest remedy was a simple, latex-free sterile adhesive bandage, but still better would be the application of a plantain leaf to squash the bleeding. Mindfully, he inched his dream catcher smoothly and quietly under his pillow for safe keeping.

Nelson wondered if his indignity would be noticed by his mother or teacher. Surely, his younger sister would see his "boo-boo," especially since three year olds seemed to focus in on such an injury. He could already hear her voice resounding in his head as she repeated the words again and again and again.

"Nelson has a boo-boo! Nelson has a boo-boo!" she would utter prolonging the long double oo's to startle him and to show her concern.

Nelson was guarded particularly for his mother's entrance into his bedroom, only because it was time to get ready for school. Time seemed to be static at that moment until the silence of the early morning bedroom was broken like a knife cutting a loaf of bread. The ring of the alarm clock made his hair stand on end, and his extremities tightened with the help of electricity that filled his nerve endings like purple fountains flowing over. As each second was measured, his hair stood taller and his nerve fibers carried impulses quickly between his brain and spinal cord and then to the other parts of Nelson's body. Lying on his back, his head slipped off the pillow as he drew his comforter up tight under his chin, like a turtle retreating into its shell. Hopefully, here he would calm his nerves and achieve some semblance calm.

R…r…r….r…ring! rang the clock, a persistent resonance throughout the room.

The vibration of the alarm was so loud that the clock danced across the top of the nightstand onto the floor, giving off a loud noise as if something was being violently broken or struck. Meanwhile, Nelson's body shot up into a sitting position, snatched up his goose down-filled pillow, and wrapped it around the circumference of his head as far as it would go.

Oh! At last!" he thought. *It wasn't completely pointless.*

Surely this activity would give him the necessary protection required to protect his hearing from the shrill sound of the bell on the top of the clock.

Clang! Clang! Clang!

It was an old-fashioned Westclox that his grandfather had purchased, where else but from The Treasure Trove during a previous trip. The hammer between the two bells seemed to move faster and faster, and the sound seemed to get louder and louder until it had almost a deafening effect. The fall from the nightstand in no way dampened its loud, intruding noise.

Next to come about was the abrupt entry by his mother. She paused briefly in the doorway that framed her body and then rushed in, allowing nothing to get in way of her hasty movements.

"Time-To-Get-Up Slugabed! It's time to get up!—How was your outing with your grandfather?"

There was no come, knock, and enter. Instead, it was more like enter. Suddenly my eyes caught a glint of light, at first it was a vexing spark, and then it lengthened when she thrust the curtains open to let the day in and life out. Grabbing the alarm clock, she turned off the clamorous sound of its ringing bells.

"What are the consequences hanging in the air for *not* getting up?" contemplated Nelson.

He'd probably find himself on restriction banished to his room for the entire month of September, a punishment worse than death. The most they could do, however, was to lock away his bike and make him walk to and from school for the remainder of the school year and forbid him to talk to Judd, one of his best friends. Any period of time separated from his bike or his friend would be a problem.

The silencing of the ring ended any further thought about such an action as he was jolted back into reality. Nelson was particularly keen to avoid trouble with his parents, especially with his mother. After all, she packed his lunch each day and *extras* were important to Nelson. He proceeded to get up, trying to remove any remaining cobwebs containing such thoughts and let out a big sigh.

"Hm................!" came the audible sound as he exhaled, giving him a feeling of relief from his weariness. This he followed with a deep, down, into the body stretch, and he was ready for the activities of the day.

As he stood at the window, the limping sun of fall peered through causing a blinding effect on Nelson's vision. Simultaneously, the ringing of the phone on the nightstand created a cacophonous sound not allowing Nelson's attention to falter over the events of a new day.

"What noise is this? The day is too young," Nelson mumbled through his heavily stuffed pillow. For a split second he hesitated. Then he breathed defiance as he swung the pillow from his head and cut the air hurting nothing, all for an attempt to get at the phone.

"*Paige here!*"

There was dead silence at the opposite end of the phone.

"*Hello! Hello! Hello!*" he called into the phone's receiver, failing to make a connection to the source. He pulled his ear away from the receiver and then pushed it tightly to his ear to drown out any surrounding noise. Finally, he was able to isolate the words coming from the voice on the other end of the phone.

"Paige. I'll meet you in ten minutes at the street corner on my bike," came a quiet voice as if he knew Nelson's mother was in the room.

"Shizznit! Shizznit!" Nelson yelled and slammed the phone down into its cradle; in the meantime, his mother had exited his room. In case you don't know, "shizznit" means that's cool in the language of Nelson and Judd.

Our thoughts create our actions that create our habits that create our character. Nelson Paige was no exception. He hadn't been in touch with his friend, Judd Levin. Events of the summer had changed Nelson Paige as Judd was soon to learn. Nelson's communication with Judd seemed estranged since he last talked to him on the final day of school before summer *recess*. It seemed more like years than months since he had last seen Judd.

Sliding down the staircase railing, Nelson made an aerodynamic delivery on the landing from his upstairs bedroom to the downstairs. Hopefully, his mother had done her weekly waxing to the stair railing to assist him in an uneventful landing. The expediency at which he slid gave him an oxygen boost ventilating his lungs, making him ready for his bike ride ahead.

Crying out of need of nutrition was Nelson's stomach, but this Monday morning it would receive no solace in the way of food from him. It would have to wait until lunch time to be nourished. The urgency to meet up with his friend, Judd, at the corner of Spencer and Maple took precedence over all else. Judd, who was one of Nelson's best friends from his neighborhood, came from an entire family of BMX bike riders. This meant he knew a whole bunch about them. For example, the Mongoose Villain was a great freestyle bike whether you are riding like a young champ or just starting out in the sport. Or that the X-Games BMX Moto bike looks like a real motor cross bike but runs on fierce power.

A quick pat on his dog Ivy's head yielded a motionless response from his dog, Ivy. For a split second he paused to check for unconsciousness. Then came a piteous, delayed bark followed by the gulping of water. This added to the empty feeling in Nelson's stomach but in a different sort of way. It wasn't because of food but the lack of affection his companion did not return. His usual lick to Nelson's hand was absent. Nelson now realized that lack of attention created a wedge between him and Ivy, which was in his estimation the long and short of it all. So, Nelson had no words for him and simply ignored him.

"Have I been that negligent?" he mumbled to himself.

Nelson was off only to back step brusquely to retrieve his brown bag lunch that his mother prepared for him daily during the school year. There it was carefully placed on the kitchen counter with a message that Nelson scanned. Scrolled with large letters was his name *Nelson*. It was the first day of the school year, and his mother had itemized the events of his day on the outside of his brown luncheon bag. Noticing that the directives were there in extra bold permanent, black Sharpie print unlike his name on the bag, conveyed a message of their importance and the need for Nelson to fulfill them step by step. The note had the likely-look of a grocery list but read in a hierarchical order of importance by numbers. Each step read like a command with "you" omitted and to be understood by its reader—*Nelson*! Unlike, a grocery list it was itemized.

Dear Nelson,

It's here, the 2nd day of September, the first day of the school year. Please note the following for the first day:

1. **No bus this year—ride your bike.**
2. **School starts at 8:00 a.m.**
3. **Turn in registration card at the "P thru R" window.**
4. **Turn in your medical forms/permission slips.**
5. **Pick up your class schedule at the "P thru R" window.**
6. **Smile for your student ID.**
7. **Report to your first period class promptly at 8:00 a.m.**

All My Best,
Mom

It struck Nelson odd that his mother seemed more apprehensive than he was about the first day of school, evident by the thicker than normal directions. This brought a broad grin to Nelson's face that remained there for what seemed like an entire minute while he contemplated her instructions and underlying intentions.

Briefly, he glanced at the clock on the wall. It now read 7:20 a.m. in large numerals on a luminous face, the perfect size for not yet open eyes. Walking to the calendar above the kitchen desk, he placed a whopping X over the seventh day of September. It was the beginning of something new, in this case a new school year. From that day on he would methodically mark each day for 180 days until that magical day in June reappeared, and spring would be in its full apparel. Then, school would be in *recess* for the summer, and Nelson loved the summer holidays, a time to be free, explore, and just plain hang out, especially with Judd. Deep in thought, Nelson slowly returned the pencil to its resting place. Particularly interesting, though not unusual for Nelson Paige, this was no time to be dreaming—school was here. Yes, school was starting, and it was time to be off—*Off and running he must go!*

CHAPTER 2

The BMX Wonder Boys

Exiting the kitchen into the garage, Nelson pressed the switch to open the garage doors. He removed his helmet from the handlebars of his bike. Positioning his Giro Flame helmet on his head, he adjusted his chinstrap for comfort and safety.

Then, unlocking his Odyssey Evolver R V-type black brake lock from his classic Spiderman BMX bike, he climbed aboard and was off to meet Judd. Riding his bike gave him a spidery feeling as he made his way to the corner of Spencer and Maple. When the sun sets, the earth drizzles dew. The morning dew that had collected on the grass had also gathered on the bike path he was traveling, leaving tracks from his place of origin. Everything about his Flame helmet assisted in his bike ride as the air rushed through its vents. It was this performance feature that sucked the air into the channeled vents of the helmet to help him move faster through the air. The air ruffled his hair, disturbing its smoothness and its regularity in pattern.

The morning haze was diminishing visibly before his eyes, and the light beyond yonder was peeking its way through the closer he came to Spencer and Maple.

Pure imagination, thought Nelson.

Momentarily, he felt like a phantom, something apparently seen, heard, or sensed but not having any physical reality—a ghost.

"What is that I feel?" Nelson asked. Some lethal pollutant intoxicated the air that surrounded him.

I feel a chill running through my bones, thought Nelson Paige.

More than likely it was a mental chill because summer was over, and school was beginning.

"Can't see it," remarked Nelson, trying to peer through the dank morning that was palpable as it touched down its moist haze to get under Nelson's skin.

As it separated, the first thing his eyes discerned was a shadowy outline. There was Judd, silhouetted on his Batman style BMX bike ready to soar into action like a nocturnal avenger relentless in his practice to perfect his tricks to be the smoothest and best possible in order to compete.

"Na nah! Na nah! Na nah! Na nah! Batman!" echoed the questioning intonation as if it was the voice of the wind. Deliberately, his voice rose and fell in pitch to contribute to its meaning as Judd hummed a snatch of the theme song from Batman.

Nelson thought he heard sounds as Judd circled around and around and around. His bike was like a bat with membranous wings. One thing was sure, his Batman style BMX maneuvered better in the rain and morning dew than his did. It seemed to suck up the moisture as he wheeled around. When Nelson was late, Judd always worked on his tricks. To keep his performance at an optimum Judd was relentless in his practice to perfect his tricks to be the smoothest and best possible in order to compete.

Judd was about to do a wheelie. Pulling back on the handlebars, he lifted the front wheel off the ground while he continued to pedal. As the bike reached the balanced point, he pushed with his arms to keep it there and continued to ride the rear wheel. Occasionally, Judd would add style to the "wheelie" by using one hand or one foot.

When Nelson came face-to-face with his friend, he came to the realization that the only thing that is constant is change—he had changed. He had been places and done things that Judd had never done or could imagine—*Or could he?*

"Hey, Judd, it's good to see you!" yelled out Nelson through the morning haze.

"You have a new trick since I saw you?"

"Come see my 'curbo endo.'"

When Judd tired of "wheelies" he would try "curb endos." He approached the curb slowly while aiming toward it as straight as possible. His body was in the seated position, and the pedals were in neutral. As the front tire touched the curb, Judd sprang upward or stood and pushed the handlebars forward with his arms. The rear of his bike lifted off the ground.

You could see the bike come up when he bended his knees. With his arms extended, he stretched back over the rear wheel. The more stretched out he was, the higher the rear wheel lifted. Judd kept his arms very stiff to keep the bike from swinging left or right. The point of the trick was to hang in the air as long as possible before gravity takes its course.

"Whoops," a short, grating cry came from Judd's lips.

You could just see how high he was because the insides of his pockets seemed to regurgitate their contents right onto the ground. And out fell in succession—a book along with his mouth, chin, and nose guard, all of which Judd found too restrictive when attempting his stunts. The book read in underlined bold black letters on a red background *Moto Racing, A Guide to International Racing*. As the book and face guard hit a chink between the stones in the concrete and landed with a loud thump, Nelson's eyes followed its landing carefully. There wasn't much movement for the book once it hit the concrete, just a distracting noise made by the spine as it hit the concrete.

"Thump!"

"Uh-oh," Nelson uttered.

On the other hand, the face guard was another story. Its red color helped to make tracking it easy as it landed, bounced, and made a hollow sound as it finally rested in the debris-filled gutter of the street. Hoping that Judd wouldn't be distracted by the fall of his pocket contents, Nelson bent his knees and threw his body forward in the direction of the landing to reclaim them for his friend.

"Ouch!" cried out Nelson with an injured expression on his clean-cut, boyish face.

Nelson flinched as he sprang upward and held his hand, trying to shake the sting from his now raw knuckles and bruised shoulder.

"A...A...A !" *hihhhhh*! his face lengthened from the discomfort it was causing him.

At the same time, he knew he could transform affliction into triumph if he focused really hard. A certain cool headedness had come to Nelson; it wasn't the first time he performed gracefully under pressure. When the general nursing of his bruised shoulder and ruptured knuckles was completed, he was again in flight. Unheeded, Nelson swiftly snatched up the face guard for safe keeping, and a grateful smile came to his lips. Despite the abrasion to his knuckles and the black and blue spots on his shoulder, Nelson had everything under control. Still better would be if Judd was wearing his face mask, this could have all been avoided. Now he had scars on both hands, like a road map to remind him of his travels. It was an unfortunate fitting end to the summer months.

"Butt-hurt," said Nelson. But much to his chagrin Judd was to the contrary. He was grateful for the actions of his friend and put his face guard on his face.

Judd was in no way distracted and continued to move forward. He liked best the part when the rear of the bike begins to drop, and he could imagine he was sitting down on eggs. As the wheel touched down, he would shift his body to the back seat. Then, he would pull back on the handlebars to begin a backward roll. Next, he would pop the front wheel off the ground, turn the handlebar left or right, do a turn on the rear wheel and pedal out of the "curbo endo."

"Do you want to see another "curbo endo?" queried Judd.

First he tried one hand followed by no hands, and then no feet.

"It looks really tight but no thank you," returned Nelson. "It was an altered version of the original by changes in rhythm.

"Nerve, Nerve, Nerve!" Nelson said panting, as he dashed along nervously. His nerves seemed a bit jumpy today.

"Oh now come on, Nelson," prodded Judd.

"I think I'll try a track stand to see if I can still do it," put forth Nelson Paige.

Perched atop his bicycle seat, Nelson came to the realization that another change had taken place over the summer. He had outgrown his bicycle and was finding difficulty in making those full circles with his feet that move the pedals to propel the wheels in a forward direction.

Yes, change is the only thing that is constant. thought Nelson Paige. The *pull* and *push* of the pedals took some adjustment to carry through the motion. Yes, Nelson had grown. It was *change* in the continuous making.

Unlike Judd Levin Nelson was only a beginner and could only do track stands or balancing tricks or poses to affect a particular attitude. He might attempt doing the "Bunny Hop," but he didn't have the attraction to the sport like Judd even though he was a much better athlete than him. Most likely his career doing BMX freestyle would end with the "Bunny Hop."

He's not bad! thought Judd Levin as he watched him in action doing the "Bunny Hop"

First, he grasped the grip of one handlebar and the seat with one hand when the front wheel was turned at ninety degrees. Next, he started out by slowly riding forward with both hands on the handlebars and stood on the pedals. He held the left pedal all the way down. Then he lifted his right leg over the top tube, and rested his right foot at the bottom of the front triangle formed by the frame or where the pedal crank joins the frame.

Using his front brake, he came to a full stop and turned his front wheel ninety degrees. With his right hand, he gripped the end of the handlebar and the seat. At the same time he moved his left foot to the front tire and released the brake as soon as his foot was in place. At this point his bike was tilted at about forty-five degrees, and his body was in the form of a rough U. Now he balanced by using his left foot to roll the front tire forward.

For the trickiest maneuver, he quickly moved his left hand from the grip to the front tire while putting his left foot back on the left pedal. He let the bike drop slightly. Using his left hand, he rolled the bike back and forth to maintain his balance.

He put all his weight on his left foot, brought his right foot up and over the top tube but under the right grip and seat. He tightened his right leg so that it was stiff, and used his right foot to lock the handlebars in place.

Then he took his hands off their respective positions and leaned back slightly. As he leaned back, the bike lifted. At this point it was crucial that Nelson did not lean completely backward. For the finale, he spread his arms out and balanced.

"Wow, Nelson!" Judd whispered as if to encourage him onward in his attempt to set down his two wheels to rest on the concrete. If only he had a camera, he would like to hold that pose for Nelson.

Unlike Judd, Nelson knew he had reached his limitations of riding in the Bicycle Moto-Cross, competition world. Judd had a conflicting idea of what was dangerous or just plain Extreme. In fact, it was an abnormal view of what was normal. Normal for Judd was Extreme. On the other hand, Nelson was content with attempting a few stunts to save face with his friend. Possibly he would add the slide stop to his repertoire, but he knew that would be the end.

Judd had a reputation as a dare devil. He loved to do "aerials" or mid-air stunts. When Judd couldn't be found, Nelson knew where to find him—at the local skateboard park. There, he would be practicing on the curved ramp or "quarter-pipe" so that he could get more height to do his mid-air stunt. Nelson loved to watch him do the "kick-turn," even though it was a standard freestyle routine.

Tricks aside, Nelson and Judd returned their bikes to the ground and were off. They biked through what seemed like an endless labyrinth of streets with genteel two-storied, brick houses that looked out in small enclosures of manicured lawns with clumps of bushes and hardy flowers planted to withstand the smoke-laden, uncongenial atmosphere.

Finally, they came to the school crossing, which was blocked with an immense stream of students and pedestrians flowing like a tide inward and outward from the entrance of the Mt. Vernon Middle School. Fifteen minutes later they were parking them in the school's bike rack and securing them with their bike locks. Suddenly the front doors to the school opened as hundreds of students filtered through them, laughing, talking, and excited to renew old friendships. The yard duty persons circulated amongst the students to thwart any scoffs that might devel.

CHAPTER 3

The Rebel Chief

"Is…Is sh…she oh n-no she…"

"I'm afraid too!" returned Nelson, as they reported into their classroom.

Judd's face looked incredulous and widened with surprise.

"I'm getting outta here," returned Judd with startled suddenness. "Get me out of this predicament," he added. Nelson sensed uneasiness in Judd's demeanor.

Because of this moment, the entire phase of Judd's life was to be affected. There stood their new teacher, not only new for the year, but new at the school. There, in perfect view, stood Ms. Woodson, the rebel chief. They'd only met, yet, instinctively he knew everything about her. There was no doubt in Judd's mind that she would rule by the laws of the school and not from her own bench. It was going to be one long year at Mt. Vernon Middle School. Judd knew she wouldn't think twice about dismissal—that is exile him to the principal's office.

"And that place had a reputation—a below standard one," thought Judd to himself.

Ms. Woodson spoke with candor, and she would definitely not try to second guess a student he was sure. He was sure that she felt it an expectation to teach the values of responsibility, respect, and safety to each and every one of her twenty-eight students.

"*He who knows the most has an obligation towards humanity,*" thought Ms. Woodson as she peered out at her anxious audience just waiting to hear her cultivated voice marked by a slight English accent that gave it precision and deliberateness.

"It is a great honor and pleasure to welcome you, boys and girls, to Mt. Vernon Middle School," said Ms. Woodson as she smiled, showing her red lips and perfectly aligned teeth.

She spoke in a low voice, almost a murmur, barely moving her lips. Her English accent was rather affected. Although over thirty, she had not lost that transparent, delicate skin that young women have before the glare of the world and their arrogance turns it to the color and feel of parchment. Enchanted by her accent, the students seemed to sit on the edge of their seats waiting to listen to her next word. She was deceptively youthful looking because of her small, slender features as delicate as an ink drawing. Her small waist highlighted her greatest quality, gracefulness. Gracefully, she moved between the rows of students and wrote on the whiteboard phrases she wanted the students to remember forever, truths to model their lives upon. As she passed the students' desks, you couldn't help but get wrapped in her scent laid down on you in a fixed way.

I know that smell. It isn't Shalimar or White Shoulders. It's more like Ponds Cold Cream that my mother uses to keep her face soft, soft as a baby's butt, thought Sydney Best. *I helped my dad shop for it for a Christmas gift.*

Both Judd and Nelson listened attentively to her. Perhaps she would reveal to them some mysteries of the feminine world—alien to both of them except for what they had learned from their sisters and mothers. And then these mysteries never extended beyond the kitchen or laundry room. Despite her young years, there she stood, formidable before them. It was time to begin to teach a lesson or two before the day expired. It was as if *fate* stepped in, tore up the script, and introduced unforeseen complications…and this year Nelson and Judd would be plunged into school life full force without any reservation. And thus as *fate* would have it, along with being *BMX Wonder Boys*, they would become *students* under the tutelage of Ms. Woodson.

The clock ticked away; however, the hands on the clock were having a difficult day. You could hear the clock ticking the seconds, minutes, and hours, but the hands were racing their way around the face of the clock—a race against time. The racing of the hands seemed to mesmerize Nelson as he watched.

That clock has the face to stop an hourglass, thought Nelson. He had a special way with puns, and today was no exception.

"Today is minimal day…I will now take attendance," echoed Ms. Woodson in her teacher voice.

As she called out each name listed alphabetically, Nelson couldn't help but notice by the whiteboard that Ms. Woodson directed strict operations in her classroom. In particular, number six stood out on her list—*You are special.* She had her lesson sequence on the whiteboard posted for the morning, not in hours, but rather minutes—four hours in all before the bell sounded to signal the end of the first day of school.

Lesson Sequence for Opening Day:
    1. Greeting and handshake   15 min.
    2. Seating Chart   10 min.
    3. Check/collect Emergency/Medical Forms/
       Permission Slips   10 mi
    4. Introductions   15 min.
    5. Classroom Expectations: 75 min.
        a. Attendance
        b. Subjects covered
        c. Course Objectives/Standards
        d. Methods of Evaluation
        e. Grading Scale
        f. Class Rules
        g. Behavior Consequences
    6. YOU ARE SPECIAL!   85 min.
    7. Dress Code   10 min.

Nelson was sure she could read his mind as she looked at him.

"No! The clock can't be stopped. The janitor needs to adjust it," Ms. Woodson responded out of nowhere with all the firmness she could muster.

Just then, Sydney Best, who he remembered from last year, began a frenetic exchange between Nelson and her. The note slipped to him while Ms. Woodson turned to the whiteboard to check her morning agenda read: *Boring*! With panic for fear of Ms. Woodson turning around in her space at that very moment, Nelson vacillated in confusion trying to decide if he should return a response in fear of the possibility of being recognized. First day in school accompanied by a note to the principal's office would not register well with his mom. Avoiding any whispers that might elicit any possible joyful giggles was probably the most prudent thing Nelson guessed.

The most interesting phase of the morning came when Ms. Woodson talked about intelligence.

"You are all very special and have special intelligences that were given to you," she said gleefully.

Hm…m…m…m! thought Nelson. *This is going to be pure torture,"* thought Judd.

"People have studied intelligence and found some of you have literary intelligence like Mark Twain or William Shakespeare. Others are logical mathematical and do arithmetic on demand like Einstein. Some of you have musical intelligence or the genius of Mozart."

"I've heard of Baby Einstein," Judd said to himself. "Yeah! Those are the tapes my mom plays to my little sister."

"Then there will be architects and engineers to demonstrate unique spatial abilities.

"Ms. Woodson…Ms Woodson!" It was Sydney Best waving her hand relentlessly trying to get the teacher's attention. "Is that like looking for hidden figures or objects in pictures?

"Yes, Sydney! How did you know?"

"Well, Ms. Woodson…Ms. Woodson, I saw a picture at an art gallery that looked like all dots. The proprietor told me to stare at it until I could see an airplane."

"Did it work, Sydney?"

"Yep! It took me the longest time. Finally, my mom had to help me. There it was, a huge jet." Sydney did come close to the dimmest crayon in the box, but then she wasn't the brightest crayon.

"Of course, we can't forget our athletes and dancers who exhibit bodily kinesthetic intelligence," continued Ms. Woodson. It was Judd's time to be heard. He stood impulsively up from his chair.

"Ms. Woodson…Ms. Woodson…like Bob Haro who created the BMX Action Trick Team."

"That's fight, Judd," confirmed Ms. Woodson.

"Finally, we have interpersonal and intrapersonal intelligence." This was more difficult for the students of this age to comprehend as Ms. Woodson could tell by the reaction of the students. There were grunts and groans and emotions associated with lack of interest. Nevertheless, the seed had been planted, only age and time would do the watering.

Judd thought for sure he was having a tumultuous dream. On the other hand, Nelson's imagination was boiling over with all this information.

"On the overhead, students, you will see symbols, and across the way are occupations. We are going to match them with the type of intelligence they require," she instructed. "Do I have any volunteers?"

Everyone volunteered, and those who didn't were very attentive. In fact, Ms. Woodson had stolen all their attentions. Seven students were chosen, and each marched to the front of the class trying to match the symbols with the proper category. Of course, the last person to go would be a no brainier. Unfortunately, Sydney was still sitting at her desk acting like she was bored with a capital B, meaning that she was really bored. As bored as any person could possibly become.

"A lick of gumption can make you a millionaire!" Nelson could hear his grandfather tell his buddies.

Gumption! Gumption! That's what I need! thought Nelson. *Yes I'll have to be brave.*

Despite the anguish of getting up in front of the room, both Nelson and Judd were chosen to participate. They were both off to a good beginning. Judd chose bodily kinesthetic intelligence because he felt comfortable with this choice. There was no BMX bike rider for the match, but there was a hockey player to place next to it. He knew he fell into this category because of his perfect awareness and control of his body. He wasn't a world class gymnast nor did he have the athletic prowess of Jerry Rice or Steve Young, but he knew he won at the BMX competitions regularly.

Nelson's feet were icy, and a shiver ran down his back. He had a faint, cold fear that ran through his veins, the kind that freezes up the heat of life. He didn't know if it was fear of what was going to happen, or the nudge by Judd to step up to the plate. In a flash of lucidity, Nelson knew that Judd would not be his ally, as he had hoped, if he didn't live up to a certain image.

"What's your IQ?" Nelson blurted out in defense of self to Judd and at the same time trying not to let his voice reveal his heart's anxiety. This question seemed to leave Judd dumbfounded. Nelson had insulted Judd's intelligence by thinking his brain pan was too small.

Nelson gravitated toward the logical mathematical characteristics of intelligence. Naturally, intelligent quotients interested him—that is the ratio of tested mental age to chronological age. Despite his love of sports, he liked to do long chains of reasoning. He loved to do physic projects and arithmetic came easily to him, unlike Judd who was overwhelmed with these types of X-tremes.

The day ended with Ms. Woodson talking about the necessity of adhering to the school dress code. When this topic was abridged, Ms. Woodson knew for sure that she would be unforgiving in her rules—a number of phone calls would be going home to parents that evening. At that point the bell sounded, and the hands on the clock seemed to take a deep breath of relief. They had stopped at 3:30 p.m.

CHAPTER 4

"One Fish! Two Fish! Red Fish! Go Fish!"

Nelson went home immediately after the noon bell rang for the first day of school. There he found his grandfather with his usual hat pulled over his frosted hair, his driven mother, his Aunt Clara, his Uncle Bernie, and, of course, his sister, Ariel, with her three friends. They were playing Euchre, a favorite pastime when lost for activity. It seemed quite unusual for them to be playing cards on a weekday—cards were played during the weekend, particularly on a Saturday night when all else failed, not on a weekday at one p.m. Their concentration on the game seemed somewhat eschew too. Uncle Bernie's conversation seemed to be on anything but the game, and Uncle Clara was complaining how Uncle Bernie spent too much money on his new car.

"I'm starved," called Nelson out to his mother with very little response.

Nelson nudged himself between his grandparents thinking that he could lower the amplitude of discord by forming a wall between them with his body; however, Aunt Clara was accustomed to wearing the breeches in their house and wasn't about to let him off easy. She was an emaciated, string bean of a lady with a very long neck that seemed to stretch longer every time she attempted to drive a point home, especially when it was directed toward Uncle Bernie.

"Now, Bernie, you know we can't afford to buy such a luxurious car at our age. It will be the death of us!" snapped Aunt Clara in her attempt to twist his wrist.

Quite the contrary, Uncle Bernie was hardly a spendthrift. Aunt Clara was just the noisiest person at this moment in the world, and to Uncle Bernie she was just plain troublesome.

Uncle Bernie only nodded and offered his smile and was not about to cook his goose in any way with Aunt Clara. Besides, it would only accelerate the premature balding of his head.

Everyone was so intent on listening to Aunt Clara that they failed to notice Nelson as he took a handful of popcorn out of their bowl.

"This is delicious. Is this kettle corn?" he asked, still without a response from anyone.

"Clubs trump!" snarled Uncle Bernie, as he moved closer to the cards and squinted to make sure he had clubs.

Sensing the lack of interest in his presence, Nelson moved in the direction of his sister, Ariel, and her three neighborhood friends.

"I wonder if my sister will start in on my hurt finger?" he questioned.

His sister might be young, but she had the memory of an elephant. She would remember his indignity.

There she was positioned around a vintage circular-hooked rug with her friends, just the way they did in preschool when they did zoo phonics. The rug was soon to become a pond for their fish game. Pulling out her own age-specific playing cards—*One Fish Two Fish Red Fish, Go Fish*—she dealt them out amongst her friends.

On a given day, an outsider would think that Ariel was related to the doll called Chatty Kathy, and today was no exception. Nonetheless, today it was Chatty Ariel as she told them about the game.

"The person with the most matching pairs wins," she informed them in her total absorption of the game.

Kathyrn, Ethan, and Anna sat tentatively waiting for instructions. As Ariel shuffled the cards, she was interrupted by Ethan pushing Anna in order to get a position in the circle. When everyone was situated,

Ariel dealt five cards face down to each of her friends. She put the remainder of the cards face down in the pond.

"I get to go first…I get to go first," said Anna as she held her hand up in the air quivering with anticipation.

"No, it's the youngest," called out Ethan with his orderly mind.

"That's me…that's me," Ariel informed the others while pointing at herself with her pointer finger.

Ariel knew the game well since she had played it many times before with her mother and sister. Only this time, her mother and sister were not there to let her win, a simple way of expressing their warmth. She liked the fish with a *Star* best, not only because of its vanity and smugness, but most of all its power.

"I know that fish is smug because of its star," she told her friends.

"That's why it's the *Wild Card*, Ariel," whispered Kathyrn.

"It's the only one with a star," whispered Anna.

"He's a pure coward. Look he's *Yellow*!" continued Ethan.

With all their thoughts about the game shared, Ariel advanced on with the game.

"Ethan, do you have a number two?" Ariel asked.

"I have a 'two' fish!" he yelled out to Ariel. He took the card and looked at the two fish with their arms positioned on their right hips as they looked at her with a cheek to cheek smile.

"Look they're posing, as if for a camera…click!" Ethan interjected on a lighter note.

"I have a match…I have a match!" yelled Ariel as she placed her cards and Ethan's match on the rug. "I get another turn…I get another turn," yelled Ariel in all her glory.

"Where is the *Star Fish*?" queried Kathyrn as play proceeded to the player on the left.

"Anna, do you have a 'red' fish!"

"One fish, two fish, red fish, go fish!" returned Anna. Now Ariel had to draw a card from the pond.

"Let me see…let me see!" called out Ethan.

"No match…I don't have a match," and Ariel placed the card into her hand. Most unusual of all the game cards were the black fish. They looked like they were small fetuses in the sixth month stage of development.

"Then it's my turn," said Ethan.

Ethan kept all his friends in the dark. He had the star fish the entire time. He was tickled stiff because any color or number he called out would be an automatic match. Everyone wanted the *Star Fish*. It gave the player unrestrained self-indulgence that resulted in pleasure.

The play continued around and around until Ariel held no more cards.

"I'm the winner…I'm the winner," sounded Ariel. She was the winner because she had the most matches, a winner she was still without her mother and sister to help.

"*If these were real fish, hopefully, they would be community fish, or it would be a feeding frenzy for sharks,*" thought Nelson as he looked at the pictures on the cards.

Ariel and her friends played the fish game frequently. When they tired of it, they moved to "The Lorax." In The Lorax, the greedy old Once-ler would cut down all of the Truffula trees. It was up to Ariel and her friends, along with the Lorax, to save them to protect the environment. Ethan was the champion of the most saves of the Truffula trees. At last, Ariel had met her match because Ethan was *always* The Lorax card winner—he was the champion of The Lorax card game. In this game everyone wanted the Bar-ba-loot card. Ethan always seemed to draw the Bar-ba-loot card, giving him the privilege to take one set of Truffula trees from any other player.

Watching them caused Nelson to reminisce about Dr. Seuss. His favorite book was *Green Eggs and Ham*, and before that he couldn't put down *The Cat and the Hat*. He could hear dimly in his mind his teacher blending the letters together ever so carefully in an attempt to get her students to read.

"C...A...T says *cat*! H...A...T says *hat*!" he said to himself. It wasn't *Ariel's Zoo Phonics* nor was it *Hooked on Phonics*, but it was successful. Dr. Seuss's immortality had extended through generations, and he still hadn't lost his charm. Unlike Nelson, Ariel loved *The Lorax* and *One Fish Two Fish Red Fish, Go Fish*.

CHAPTER 5

Surprise! Surprise!

Nelson's thoughts were soon brought back to his present consciousness when he heard sounds of "Happy Birthday" being sung. Slowly he rotated around; there in the doorway was Sydney, Judd, and a number of other classmates from Mt. Vernon Middle School all in a twitter.

Unharmonious close quarters between Aunt Clara and Uncle Bernie over his new car came to a sudden halt when they saw Ms. Woodson come waltzing into the kitchen with a most unusual hat.

"My teacher at my house! How can this be?" questioned Nelson as he whipped around in disbelief. "*Surely, it had to be a bad dream,*" he pondered in quiet anticipation.

"It can't be?" whispered Nelson's mother. She had never seen her before except at Back to School Night.

Crowning her reddish-brown hair was an extra tall hat surmounted with twelve irregular in height birthday candles of assorted colors. It was probably something she purchased from the Mad Hatter's shop on one of her visits to a theme park. It fit the spirit of the occasion; however, it left Nelson cemented in his footsteps with his mouth agape in a condition of wonderment and surprise. Ms. Woodson even brought a smile to Aunt Clara's otherwise grim face.

The secret was out. It was Nelson's *surprise* party; Ms. Woodson let the cat out of the bag.

"What games are we going to play?" asked Aunt Clara nervously. "If you don't pay attention to this, we are going to create obsessive-compulsive people."

Just the idea of introducing activities ruled by resistant ideas, irresistible impulses, or both made Aunt Clara even more nervous.

"Don't worry, Aunt Clara. Now don't you worry! Everything is under control," Nelson's mother in her attempt to produce a feeling of serenity into the room knew the games needed to be not too structured to allow the players to negotiate relationships with their peers.

Nelson's mother had considered several points before making the selection of games for the party, like the number the classmates invited were sixteen, there were eight boys and eight girls, indoor games, time enough for one game to be played before the opening of presents and the remainder after presents were opened. The old favorite games would be saved for last, especially for those classmates who were new to Nelson's class this year.

Being creative was what Nelson's mom enjoyed most. For the birthday party she drew the games to be played on the outside of a balloon as follows

1. Advanced Fortune

2. Wonder Ball

3. Marble Roll Away

4. Crazy Auction

5. Gold Digging

6. Indoors Hunt

Nelson's mother waved her hand furiously at Aunt Clara to stop throwing negatives at Uncle Bernie and at the same time attempted to save face for the entire Paige family. Aunt Clara was notorious for cutting off her nose to spite her face, or some of you might understand it better if I said she was always sticking her foot in her mouth. Since it was her sister, she could get away with trying to get her ruffled feathers to lie down.

There followed the lighthearted sound of voices associated with the merriment of a party.

Pop! Pop!

Dozens of balloons clung to the walls by means of static electricity to announce something about to happen.

There's going to be a party?" informed Grandfather.

Partygoers were grabbing them and pushing them between the palms of their hands. The noise of the balloons popping could be heard throughout the room. It created a room full of excitement and laughter and festivity.

"I got you…I got you…I got you!" echoed between party blowers as they blew their party blowers into other people's faces.

Streamers and confetti were thrown into the air and could be found in every cranny in the furniture, the pockets of their clothes, and throughout their hair. Hats of every style and different sizes and shapes were flopped upon heads.

And then the noise level came to a low when a fresh sheet cake with whipped cream frosting and a red script saying, "Congratulations Nelson Paige, A Fine Boy of Twelve Years," was placed on the table. Straight in the center of the script was a BMX rider doing a "wheelie." Surrounding the biker were pennants made from lollipop sticks. Tiny flags were cut from colored construction paper. Carefully, it was positioned in the middle of the kitchen table for all to see.

"*Life is complete for this moment,*" thought Nelson as he looked at the "*surpassingly*" good looking cake.

Next to the cake was the menu to be served before the cake and the pennant ice cream made from a pint brick of Neapolitan ice cream.

Each slice had a layer of chocolate, vanilla, and strawberry ice cream. Since ice cream and cake are standard fare at almost any "party, it would be served at the end of the party.

"Serve-yourself" style was for the main refreshments. One sure success was a soda fountain set up where Nelson's classmates could concoct their own wildest sodas, along with a menu to choose their favorite foods.

MENU
Round-the-World Hot Dog
BMX Hamburger
Baked Beans
Potato Chips/Potato Salad
Pickles
Double Chocolate Cake
Pennant Ice Cream

It was only the beginning of what was to follow. Aunt Clara loosened up, and Uncle Bernie brought his fist downward on the table as if to signal to the others.

Let the party begin!

The incident brought an inundation of tears of laughter to Nelson's eyes. Then Uncle Bernie, who possessed minute knowledge on every subject, shook with laughter. He raised the thicket of his eyebrows, puffed out his chest with the appearance of little pride, mopped his forehead, and announced the reason for his visit as his left eye fluttered down into a wink.

"To celebrate the day in the life a fine young man," he bellowed as if to make the entire room shake, "To celebrate Nelson's thirteenth birthday. It's not every day a young boy turns thirteen." An extraordinary and curt announcement delivered on the part of Uncle Bernie.

Laughter shook Nelson's uncle as he looked with his small, fat-encircled eyes and nodded in his direction while crossing his arms on his hogshead of a chest. Out of his tight fist he produced a crisp fifty dollar bill with Grant on it. From that point on the presents didn't stop until the last gift was opened. There was one opened… and then another present…and another present…and another…and another… followed by silence. Last was Nelson's dad rolling in a new BMX bike exhibiting one of those ear to ear grins. He clapped Nelson on the shoulder and handed the bike over. Even Aunt Clara shrieked, followed by Nelson putting up with her hugs and a large kiss planted on his cheek.

CHAPTER 6

Advanced Fortunes

"Time to play Advanced Fortunes," announced Nelson's mom.

How! How! How did she know my thoughts? Nelson questioned.

"Aunt Clara, will you pass out the paper and pencils?"

Oh what will my fortune be? wondered Nelson. *Or will I be fortune's fool?"*

"Oh Happy Day! It's Nelson's birthday!" sounded Nelson's grandfather over and over. "Then fill in only your name where it says name."

Name: **Another color:**

Boy/Girl Name: **Job:**

Year: **Place:**

Number: **Game:**

Color:

All fourteen of the partygoers joined into a circle to fill out their pieces of paper.

"Now fold down the papers so that just your names are covered," instructed Nelson's mom. "Would someone collect them?

"I'll collect the papers," volunteered Grandfather, and then he mixed them well.

"Pass them out again," directed Nelson's mom. "Now those people who have G's, write a boy's name next to the G who is at the party today. Those of you who have B's, write a girl's name. who is at the party today.

"Now fold down the papers to cover the response and pass the papers one person to the right. Continue to fold and pass for each new item on the list. When you have filled in the space 'Game,' give them to Aunt Clara."

Nelson's mom then read them aloud, starting with the birthday boy's fortune first.

Name: *Nelson*
Boy/ Girl Name: *Sydney (B)*
Year: *2020*
Number: *6,749*
Color: *Pink*
Another color: *Green*
Job: *Jockey*
Place: *Hawaii*
Game: *Jump Rope*

As fortune had it "Nelson married Sydney in 2020. They have 6,749 children with pink eyes and green hair. He is a jockey; they live in Hawaii. They play jump rope all day long."

What a fortune! thought Nelson *--such a wild and farfetched fortune.* No prize was necessary for the game. The fortunes were a *reward* in themselves.

Ivy was also included in the celebration. She expressed his wishes by spreading his drool all over the kitchen floor then lying on her back to make like a hot dog. Only when Nelson rubbed his stomach pretending to add the relish and mustard did he assume an erect position. Nelson smiled jovially as he returned to lapping water in the corner from her bowl.

At last, at long last came the videos—videos of he and Judd doing aerials. Everyone watched intently as many attempted to eat their second piece of birthday cake.

"*Delectable!*" blurted out Sydney.

"*Dee lek tuh bul!*"

"Heah! What does that mean?" Judd quizzed with his ears perking up. "It sounds like '*Do lick the bowl.*'"

"No, silly," rebutted Sydney Best. "It means that it's delicious. You're a duffer, Judd," added Sydney as she moved her pointer finger in a circular motion pointed at her temple. "Delicious is delicious!" she responded savoring each bite of the birthday cake.

Aunt Clara sipped her coffee with her pinkie sticking out. Ariel and her friends continued to entertain themselves with the balloons while watching the bike tricks attempted by Nelson and Judd on the video screen

"Aah!" said Aunt Clara. "What a good nephew we have. I love to see healthy young men."

Leaning against the wall aloof and breathing heavily, Nelson tried to remember the jumps he was attempting. It was really Judd who was the star, but it wasn't his birthday so people didn't notice.

The last surprise came from the least expected person in the room—Sydney Best. At first her present brought a chuckle to Nelson, and then he picked it up. He guessed it to be a book on BMX riding—but it wasn't. The suspense was too great. He grabbed it and ripped off the birthday wrap. His heart skipped a beat when he found two tickets to the BMX nationals. He had to struggle not to whoop with joy.

"*Wow* Sydney!" he said, "You are the *best*. The only thing better would be to participate in the nationals." There was no doubt in his mind that this was Judd's goal, but with his new BMX bike time would change everything.

The only thing that is constant is change, thought Nelson Paige

CHAPTER 7

Indoor Treasure Hunt

The games continued until the last one was played. By far the first game, "Advanced Fortune," and the final game, "Indoor Treasure Hunt," were winners with Nelson's friends.

For the final game Nelson's mom had prepared riddles for each team of the fourteen partygoers.

A.
Red, black, yellow, green
You need them in a stream
Comes rain or snow
You'll need them wherever you go.

B.
Kerosene or electric, they may be, \\\\\\
No matter they help you see,
From dawn to dusk
They rhyme with camp and are a must.

C.
"_____ _____ on the wall,
who is the fairest of us all?" asked
the wicked one of Snow White fame.

D.
They hold the key to every door.
And can be identified by numbers,
Doors usually have one and no more,
A key in them protects you when its time to slumber.

E.
Your friends may be far,
But you can make them feel near,
Unlike the farthest star,
When their voice you hear.

F.
When I'm tired at the end of day,
Hard, soft, tall, or small,
In them my body falls,
To gather the relaxation and comfort they pay.

G.
I'm a set of written sheets, a set of blank sheets,
or a set of printed sheets.
I'm gathered between covers.
I'm sometimes found in volumes
I'm found in libraries for you to enjoy.

H.
What time is it?

They made one complete set of riddles (A-H) for each team. Each riddle was lettered in the upper left-hand corner. The answers to the riddles were left blank only Aunt Clara and Nelson's mom knew the answers. Next, Nelson's mom with the help o Aunt Clara drew up a chart. Each team of partygoers was identified by Roman numerals (I-VII

I	II	III	IV	V	VI	VII
A-1	B-1	C-1	D-1	E-1	F-1	G-1
B-1	G-2	F-2	E-2	D-2	A-2	C-2
C-3	A-3	G-3	B-3	F-3	E-3	D-3
D-4	E-4	A-4	G-4	C-4	B-4	F-4
E-5	C-5	D-5	F-5	A-5	G-5	B-5
F-6	D-6	B-6	A-6	G-6	C-6	E-6
G-7	F-7	E-7	C-7	B-7	D-7	A-7
H-8	H-8	H-8	H-8	H-8	H-8	H-8

Each team was given seven riddles and one clue that they must solve. The riddles must be answered according to the sequence on the chart. As you solve the riddle, whisper the answer into Aunt Clara's ear who will tell Nelson's mom. If the answer is correct, the bell will ring signaling the team to move on to the next riddle. You have thirty minutes to solve seven riddles and answer the final clue. The winner is the first team to do this. This team will be the winner of the Treasure Hunt.

One of the players was still finishing his piece of birthday cake so Nelson PaigeThe filled in his place with Sydney Best as his teammate. Another team stopped at Riddle E to sit in a chair. The sound of the bell to announce one more riddle had been solved echoed through out the room causing a frenzy in the room to get to the final clue.

"O Happy Day! What a great day this is," said Grandfather as he watched the partygoers in search of the treasure.

"And the winner of the Treasure Hunt is Team II. Judd Levin and Tara Pembroke," announced Nelson's mom to the partygoers as she handed them tickets to the movie *Spiderman*.

Answers to the riddles:

Riddle A. boots	**Riddle E. cell phone**
Riddle B. lamp	**Riddle F. chair**
Riddle C. mirror, mirror	**Riddle G. book**
Riddle D. keyhole	**Riddle H. Treasure slip under wristwatch!**

Clara took nine envelopes and labeled them as follows:

No. 1: Not to be hidden; to be given to the children at start of the game
No. 2: To be hidden: inside or around *boots*
No. 3: To be hidden: around *lamps*
No. 4: To be hidden: around *mirrors*
No. 5: To be hidden: around *keyholes*
No. 6: To be hidden: around *telephones*
No. 7: To be hidden: around *chairs*
No. 8: To be hidden: around *books*
No. 9: To be hidden around *wristwatch*

Next she placed the slips of paper containing the clues in the proper packages.

The clues were hidden in the morning of the party after Nelson left for school, which explained Nelson's mom's quick exit from his room after she threw open the curtains. One envelope at a time was taken following the directions on the outside. The success of the final game of the party came down to all the advanced preparations by Nelson's mom and Aunt Clara.

"If it says *lamp*, try to use more than one lamp to keep the clue areas from becoming congested. Fold each clue and hide it so that just the edge of the paper shows from the hiding place. Oh yes, save the envelope number one until you are ready to begin the game!" directed Nelson's mom.

It was now time to play the final game of the party. Aunt Clara gave each player one clue from the envelope number one. Then Nelson's mom read out the instructions to play the hunt:

1. Give each player one clue from envelope number one. Each player must find seven more clues before he comes to the treasure.

2. Each player has a different Roman numeral on the top of his clue. During the hunt, you may use *only* the clues bearing the same Roman numeral as his own. If you should find a clue with a different Roman numeral on it, you must quickly fold it up again and place it exactly where it was before. *It is important that you do this or the game will be ruined.*

3. Everyone, read your first clue. Now you are ready to begin the search for clue number two. Don't be concerned about the letters of the alphabet that appear in the upper left-hand corners of each clue. Those letters are not important and were just put there to help us in setting up the game. Your concern is only the

numbers from one to eight in the upper right-hand corners.

4. As your friends find clue number two, you may wish to check to be sure they have the right one. You may need to help some of the players to read the more difficult words in the clues. Be sure not to give away the hiding place in doing so!

5. You need to wait for your other classmates to catch up before going on to clue number three. The first person to find the slip, *'You have found the treasure!'* must be sure that he has all his clues in order. That person will then receive the treasure (prize).

Apart from his school friends, the only thing that Nelson thought about was his blood brother, Beaver-Tail. How strange he would have thought a birthday party was in the life of a young boy turning thirteen. Nevertheless, Nelson had a birthday treasure forever.

CHAPTER 8

The Dream Catcher

Nelson was down to his last guest before he lowered himself down into the sofa situated directly opposite the fireplace. He was exhausted from the party, There he sat quiet, recollecting what had come to pass. Sorting out the layers of emotions that go with the festivities of a party, he could feel the palpitation of his heart beat faster and faster and faster.

Thump! Thump! Thump!

After his last farewell, an inclination overtook Nelson as he peered at his new BMX bike sitting in the corner of the room. The thought of trying out his new bike was becoming a fixation with him, and fixations can be stubborn. It was burrowing into his brain and affecting his attitude; consequently, the thought needed to be nixed. Not for the life of him would social conventions permit him to exit hastily his guest at that moment, especially since it was—you guessed it Uncle Bernie. After all, he did come to his party and brought him a gift.

Soon, boredom began to weigh on Nelson like a heavy coat of armor. For a brief moment he felt like a knight and the next a daredevil. He swept back a strand of his hair that had fallen in his face with the back of his hand and wiped perspiration that had collected upon his brow.

He escaped from his crashing ennui through the gentle patting of his dog, Ivy. It seemed to slow the palpitations of his heart. As he patted, he couldn't help but turn a careful eye once again on his Uncle Bernie. He looked like a Scottish games participant. His physique was punctuated by his barreled chest, but he was thin in the pins. He lacked elegance, which so interfered with Aunt Clara's image of him and accounted for her quick delivery of impressions not in his favor. His ruddy face was topped with a mass of salt-and-pepper curls that added up to a rather vulgar whole. It was only when he opened up his mouth to inspire the world with his ideas and the torrent of his voice that he transformed into an entirely different form of creation. He seemed to grow to new heights while his potbelly was sucked up into the cavern of his chest. His face took on a new presence of mind and was filled with jubilance. One more *tête-à-tête* with Aunt Clara would have been too much.

Before their departure Uncle Bernie and Aunt Clara rose to their feet, supporting one another, stumbling, they approached Nelson to retire him to his room. Terrified with the inevitable, and with no idea how, they walked with him down a long corridor in darkness, climbed a short staircase, and reached his room. His name in Greek Courier letters marked his bedroom door. Entering into his cluttered room, they discovered electronic equipment, furniture, and dusty, sweaty uniforms where they had been left for the first time only two days before. Nestled against the far wall sat an elaborate computer work station—a flat screen video monitor with speakers, two hard drives, a multi-channeled audio console, and two towers. They drew shut the same window covering that Nelson's mother was so quick to open that very same morning to the tune of—*"Time-To-Get-Up-Slugabed! It's Time to Get Up!"*

They sank into the refuge of the darkness, recovering their breath from the climb of the stairs. The threesome was unable to articulate a single word. At that moment, Nelson was about to experience another side of his Olympic uncle and his string bean Aunt.

Nelson retired to his bathroom to remove his clothes in preparation for bedtime. Upon returning, on the surface his Aunt and Uncle seemed as they always had been, but their exchanges with him before tucking him in for the evening were filled with perfect composure. He immediately erased from his mind the disenchantment of Aunt

Clara's mood what seemed like constant carping at his Uncle Bernie. For the moment, he relegated them to a sealed compartment of peace, tranquility, and happiness.

Nelson pulled the coverlet back and pushed his pillow into a comfortable position before wondering the whereabouts of his aunt and uncle who had made an expedient exit down the stairs, leaving Nelson alone. The Westclox on the bedside now registered nine p.m., and the streets outside were deserted with huge shadows being cast from the houses illuminated from the moon. No lights shone from any of the houses, only the twinkling of the street lights.

"See you later!" intonated their voices in unison. Nelson did a double take while returning an expression of disbelief at the now joining forces.

Resting his head ever so gently upon his pillow, a funny prickling on the back of his neck made Nelson feel uncomfortable. Slowly, he pulled himself upward into a sitting position, his hand inching itself under the pillow. Locating the dream catcher, he wrapped his finger around it.

"Ouch!"

He was quick on the trigger to remove his hand with the dream catcher in his clutches only to discover a rough edge from the bent willow. Carefully, he twirled it around and placed it close to his face looking through the webbing of sinew. The merchant at the Treasure Trove said the dream catcher was hung from a baby's cradleboard or near the sleeping area. It was believed to sort dreams. The bad dreams were caught in the web, while the good dreams flowed through to the dreamer. Nelson quickly placed it back under his pillow so as not to prick his neck.

Extinguishing the light of the room left only the illumination of his alarm clock. Though the light was limited, it did not in any way prevent Nelson from dreaming. Everyone is born with some special talent, and Nelson discovered early on that his was to dream—to have a vision. The things we forget may well as never happened, but Nelson had many memories, both real and illusory, and that was like living twice. This was a gentle night of his childhood when the contours of reality were faint. He was about to enter a place of dreams along a much traveled path of another culture and time and would return very carefully in order not to shatter the feeble visions against the harsh light of consciousness. At any rate, a dream was about to take place.

According to the legend of the Dream Catcher, Native Americans of the Great Plains believe the air is filled with both good and bad dreams. The good dreams pass through the center hole to the sleeping person. The bad dreams are trapped in the web, where they perish in the light of dawn.

The dream catcher was performing its magic by sorting out Nelson's dreams, dreams of the past as far back as 1860s in the culture of the Plains Indians. All his bad dreams like Aunt Clara's carping at Uncle Bernie were collecting in the webbing of sinew. In contrast, Nelson's good dreams were filtering through the dream catcher. The dream catcher took him far and wide. The more he focused in, the more he was able to enter into the Great Spirit along with the Plains People. The Great Spirit had power over all things—the animals, the vegetation that sprung from the earth, and the clouds that swept the sky. Nelson was about to enter into a vision, a gift from the spirits.

In his dream he met Buffalo Calf who made his home with his mother, Buffalo Woman, and his Uncle, Buffalo Hide in a village on a high bluff. There was no forest surrounding the village, only cottonwoods and willows growing along its shores.

Oh! I can still see those balls of cotton flying through the air and landing in my hair and covering my clothes, said Nelson to himself.

He couldn't forget the cottonwood his grandparents had in their yard that each year seemed to cover the earth, surrounding the tree in a soft, white blanket. They stuck to everything they contacted.

In his dream he saw gentle rolling hills covered with grass. They gave the appearance of the great swelling or surging of waves in the sea. To Nelson the sun skipped about in the grass as if to tease. The wind seemed to occupy itself in amusement in sport or recreation while the clouds with hues between violet and red raced between the empty spaces above, like an eagle with outstretched wings soaring in the flight.

Nelson pushed himself closer to the dream catcher. This time he saw a village, and in the center was a large, round open space where the dance ceremonies were held. Unlike Nelson's worldview of progressive straight line, Buffalo Calf's was an endless circle. The cyclical nature of his existence was reflected both in the natural world itself, with its changing seasons, and the repeated cycles of birth, death, and rebirth.

"I am Buffalo Calf, Sioux Indian. I am not Cheyenne or Arapaho but Sioux."

"I am Nelson Paige, thirteen-year-old."

"Come dance," offered Buffalo-Calf.

The houses were not of bark wick-i-ups, {no change} but earth lodges, ring on ring of them. They served as an enclosure or boundary for the ceremonial ground. The side of the town toward the plains was hemmed in by a tall wall of posts driven some distance into the earth. Into the posts were cut openings like windows through which arrows could be released at any imposing enemy that might appear. Platforms were placed strategically to climb onto to get a better view. On the edge of the bluff there was no wall. The steep sides of the cliff prevented enemies from scaling them. Down below was the river bottom where the gardens were located with tall swaying corn and other vegetables.

"Come join pow-wow," said Buffalo Calf.

"What's a pow-wow?" asked Nelson Paige.

"Time for my people to get together to sing, dance, feast, play, and story tell," continued Buffalo Calf. "First I go to sweat lodge."

CHAPTER 9

The Sweat Lodge

Religious ceremonies played a very important part in the lives of Buffalo Calf and the Plains People. They had ceremonies to honor the Great Spirit. Ceremonies were held toname a baby, for a girl's coming of age, a boy's first hunt, marriage, death, the sun and many more. Before a public ceremony or a private ritual, Buffalo Calf or other tribesmen would restrict themselves to a sweat lodge for spiritual and physical purification. Insulated was a small hut covered with bark, blankets, or mats. Men entered the lodge, sweated in the stream, then ran out and plunged into a nearby stream or river.

As soon as the Plains People became possessed of the Messiah idea, they organized the Messiah or Ghost Dance, and this was taken in charge by the medicine men. One man was appointed "High Priest" to have entire control of the ceremonies. His four assistants were like wise invested with power to start or stop the dance at will. They were given authority to punish any person who should refuse to obey their commands.

While the priest were employed in their prayers, the squaws made a good sized sweat hours. Poles were stuck in the ground, and the tops bent together and securely tied. These saplings are strong enough to bare the weight of several hundred pounds.Over the framework are heaped blankets and robes to such a thickness that no smoke or steam could pass from the interior. A fire was started in a hole in the ground several feet from the small entrance to the sweat lodge, twenty or thirty good sized stones placed therein to be heated. When these rocks had sufficiently heated, the young men partook in the bath strip.

With the exception of the breech clout, they crawled through the door. They sat themselves in a circle, with their feet toward the center and their backs against the sides of the lodge. The attendant shoved some of the hot stones inside, and the young men poured water from a hide bucket upon the little stone heap. Steam and vapor arose, completely filling the enclosure. The attendant had meanwhile covered the opening so that no air from the outside would penetrate. As the vapor condenses, the attendant thrust more stones within, and thus the operation was continued as long as the youth could stand the confinement.

The pipe was also smoked during the sweat. When the young men left from their bath, the perspiration was streaming from every pore. It if was not cold weather, they plunged into a pool in the creak near by, but I it was chilly, they wrapped blankets about their bodies.

Several sweat houses were erected in order to prepare the young men for the dances. When a good number of young men, say fifty or sixty, had thus prepared themselves, the high priest and his assistants came forward. The high priest wore eagle feathers in his hair, and a short skirt reached from his waist nearly to his knees. The dancers wore no ornaments, and entered the circle without their blankets. Many of them wore only their ordinary clothes.

Dancing without trappings, which they so dearly loved, proved conclusively that some powerful religious influence is at work. The candidates for "conversion" do not fast. After they came forth from the sweathouse, they are ready to enter the sacred circle. The high priest ran quickly from the village to the open space of ground, five or six hundred yards distant, and, stationing himself near the sacred tree he began his chant as follows:

"Hear, hear you all persons! Come, hurry up and dance, and when you have finished forming the circle, tell these people what you have seen in the spirit land. I myself have been in the spirit land and have seen many strange and beautiful things, all of which my eyes tell me are good and true."

As the speaker proceeded, the men and women left their tepees and crowded to the dance ground. They formed two or three circles, according to the number of persons who wished to participate, and, grasping hands with fingers interlocked, the circles began to move toward the left. They rubbed their palms in dust or sand to prevent slipping, for it is considered unlucky to break connections.

The sacred tree is a straight sapling thirty or forty feet high, trimmed of branches to a height of several feet. To the topmost twigs is attached a small flag or canvas strip, supposed to be an emblem of purity, together with some colors. The base of the tree is wrapped with rushes and flags to a thickness of about five feet. Between the reeds the dancers from time to time thrust little gifts or peace offerings. These offerings are supposed to allay the anger of the Great Spirit and were given in perfectly good faith by the poor natives. They consisted of small pieces of calico, bags of tobacco, or pipes.

As the circle moved toward the left, the priest and his assistants cried out loudly for the dancers to stop a moment. As they paused, he raised his hands toward the west, and, upon all the people acting similarly, began the following remarkable prayer:

"Great Spirit, look at us now. Grandfather and Grandmother have come. All these good people will someday join Wakantanka, but they will be brought safely back to earth. Everything that is good you will see there, and you can have all these things by going there. All things that you hear there will be holy and true, and when you return you can tell your friends how spiritual it is." As Hiawatha was the great deliver of the Iroquois, Wakantanka was the great deliver of the Sioux.

As he prayed, the dancers cry aloud with all the fervor of religious fanatics. They moaned and sobbed, many of them exclaiming: "Great Father, I want you to have pity upon me!"

The breasts of the worshippers heaved with emotion; they groaned and cried as if they were suffering great agony; and as the priest begged them to ask great Wakantanka to forgive their sins, such a cry of despair and anguish arose.

After prayer and weeping and offerings had been made to the sacred pole, the dance was started again. The dancers went rather slowly at first, and as the priests in the center began to shout and leap about, the dancers partook of the enthusiasm. Instead of moving with a regular step, each person jumped backward and forward, up and down, as hard as he or she could without relinquishing his hold upon his neighbor's hand. One by one the dancers fall out of the ranks, some staggering like drunken men, others wildly rushing here and there almost bereft of reason. Many fell upon the earth to writhe about as if possessed by demons, while blinded women threw their clothes over their heads and ran through brush or against trees. The priests were kept busy waving eagle feathers in the faces of the most violent worshipers. The feather was considered sacred, and its use, together with the mesmeric glance and motion of the priest, soon causes the victim to fall into a trance or deep sleep.

When the "converts" came out of the trance they frequently claimed to have seen glorious visions, to have visited heaven, and to have talked with the Messiah. Little Arrow related his experience as follows:

"When I fell in the trance a great and grand eagle came and carried me over a great hill, where there was a village. The teepees were all of buffalo hides, and we made use of the bow and arrow, there being nothing of white man's manufacture in the beautiful land. The broad and fertile lands stretched in every direction, and were most pleasing to my eyes. "I was taken in the presence of the great Messiah, and he spoke to me these words:

'My child, I am glad to see you. Do you want to see your children and relations who are dead?'

'Yes, I would like to see my relations who have been dead a long time.'

The God then called my friends to come up to where I was. They appeared, riding the finest horses I ever saw, dressed in superb and most brilliant garments, and seeming very happy. As they approached, I recognized the playmates of my childhood, and I ran forward to embrace them while the tears of joy ran down my cheeks.

We all went together to another village, where there were very large lodges of buffalo hide, and there held a long talk with the great Wakantanka. Then he had some squaws prepare us a meal of herbs, meat, wild fruits, and 'wasna' (pounded beef and choke-cherries). After we had eaten, the Great Spirit prayed for our people upon the earth, and then we all took a smoke out of a fine pipe ornamented with the most beautiful feathers and porcupine quills. Then we left the city and looked into a great valley where there were thousands of buffalo, deer, and elk feeding.

"After seeing the valley, we returned to the city, the Great Spirit speaking meanwhile. He told me that the earth was now bad and worn out; that we needed a new dwelling place. He further instructed me to return to my people, the

Sioux, and say to them that if they would be constant in the dance he would shortly come to our aid. If the high priests would make for the dancers medicine shirts and pray over them, no harm could come to the wearer; that any bullets shot to stop the Messiah Dance would fall to the ground without doing anyone harm, and the person firing such shots would drop dead. He said that he had prepared a hole in the ground filled with hot water and fire for the reception of all non-believers. With these parting words I was commanded to return to earth."

Filled with the strange new hope inspired by such language, the Plains People eagerly adopted the new doctrine, and now famous, "Messiah Craze." Unfortunately, it led to tragic events and policies resulting in suffering and death in the days to come.

Nelson Paige soon learned that the Sun Dance was a very important ceremony among the Plains People. It was performed to gain supernatural power or to fulfill a vow made to a divine spirit in return for special help.

"We do dance to invoke the sun. Sun necessary to make the grass grow," contributed Buffalo Calf." "/Sun Dance performed to gain power.

Nelson began to move his body in a rhythmic way to the music.

"Stay in space," said a dancer to Nelson Paige.

Nelson Paige soon discovered that the Sun Dance was an annual ceremony for the Plains People. For three to four days, dancers gathered around a central pole with a buffalo skull on top of it.

"Pole represent east/west axis of the world," added Buffalo Calf, pointing first to the east and then to the West.

Nelson watched tentatively as skewers were tied to the central pole and then through the chest muscles of the dancers, who then danced until the skewers pulled loose. Nelson learned that he was required to stay in his own space to release his energy in the same way that the other dancers remained in their spaces. In their spaces each dancer expressed his appreciation to the stars, the sun, which is the center of the earth.

"Thanks for sustaining our life with your light and heat" came the words expressed through emotion by releasing energy through the delight in movement.

After the ceremonial dance Nelson joined Buffalo Calf in one of the lodges of the Plains People. To Nelson, they were huge mounds of earth. It was summer, and they were covered with grass.

"In winter large bumps of white," declared Buffalo Calf.

To the naked eye they would be disguised; however, they had plumes of gray smoke ascending from them, announcing the inhabitants within. The mounds were like overturned bowls lined with poles and posts.

"Watch head. Do not hit," Buffalo Calf said to Nelson Paige.

Nelson walked through a short, slanting, earth-covered tunnel and stepped down to the floor. Immediately, he noticed the circular room with a ring of tall posts at the outer edge of the floor. Between and behind these posts were the family's tools and furniture.

"Come see!" beckoned Buffalo Calf.

Nelson watched as Buffalo Calf carefully pointed out and in some cases handed hoes of buffalo shoulder blades, corn planting sticks, rakes of elk antlers, poles, piles of firewood, wooden mortars for pounding corn into meal, and platforms for storing food.

"What's this?" asked Nelson when he happened upon bull boats for crossing the rivers. "They look like giant bowls."

"We make frames from willow and cover with buffalo hide," exchanged Buffalo Calf. "You sleep here,"

Nelson Paige noticed the beds were around the room between the posts.

"Raise beds between posts. Raise off the floor on willow slats and make skin tent for protection," said Buffalo Calf.

"It looks like a big shoe box," returned Nelson Paige. Nelson Paige's eyes were immediately drawn to what appeared to be an altar.

"Family altar contains sacred medicine of family totems," contributed Buffalo Calf.

CHAPTER 10

Chicken Soup

"Come, join me at pit!" said Buffalo Calf to Nelson.

Upon arriving in the center of the room in a square formed by four upright posts, a fire burned in a shallow pit. There sat Mother Buffalo Woman making moccasins, Grandfather Tooth-Broken-In-The-Middle with his back to a draft shield making arrows. Uncle Buffalo Hide shared a story with them.

This Earth Is Precious

You must teach your children that the ground beneath their feet is the ashes of your grandfathers. So that they will respect the land, tell the children that the earth is rich with the lives of our kin.

Teach your children what we have taught our children, that the earth is our mother.

Whatever befall the earth befalls the sons and daughters of the earth. If man spit upon the ground, he spits upon himself.

This we know: The earth does not belong to man; Man belongs to the earth. This we know.

All things are connected, like the blood that unites our family.
All things are connected.

Whatever befalls the earth befalls our sons and daughters of the earth. Man did not weave the web of life; he is merely a strand in it. Whatever he does to the web, he does to himself.

With the story completed, Buffalo Calf left abruptly his seat at the fire and ran up through the door tunnel and climbed to the roof on a ladder, which was just a log with notches cut into it. He clambered up to the smoke hole on top and looked back down into the house. There was Buffalo Woman, all bent over stewing elk ribs and stirring corn mush. Then he could turn his eyes to the village circle on the outside, where women were busy bringing bundles of firewood, where warriors were huddled talking over the affairs of the day, and where children and dogs tumbled about in a game of tag.

Nelson Paige found himself being taught a gambling game by Grandfather Tooth-Broken-In-The-Middle for great concentration called hand, stick, and bone. Each of them chose his team. While singing and gesturing as a distraction, one side secretly pass a marked pebble, stick, or bone between teammates, and the other teammates had to guess who had it. The game continued for many hours before Grandfather Tooth-Broken-In-The-Middle had to tend to the business of survival.

A variety of games were played by the Plains People to develop speed, endurance, and coordination. There was the sacred hoop game and stickball, played by the men, and shinny, played by the women. All required getting a ball across a goal line. On a less competitive note, in the winter boys would go like the wind on sleds made of buffalo rib cages. Girls played house with miniature tepees and cornhusk dolls. Adults and children enjoyed singing, dancing, and storytelling around a fire on cold nights.

Still farther down the river Buffalo Calf could see the cornfields and the girls stacking the driftwood along the riverbank. As he looked at the river bend stretch across the Great Plains, it called images of a lazy snake moving across the Great Plains as it, too, bent and squirmed forward.

"We not wander all year," informed Grandfather Tooth-Missing-In-The Middle to the others. "We live in the lodges and tend gardens."

Buffalo Calf and the others had peace of mind because they knew their fort walls were their protection from outside invaders

"It is summer, and it is time to wander for buffalo for winter," instructed Grandfather Tooth-Broken-In-The Middle.

Buffalo Calf and the Plains People knew a long walk was ahead of them since they did not have horses.

"We jerk buffalo and elk meat, winter food," added Tooth-Broken-In-The-Middle.

"I help lash teepees and belongings to travois," offered Buffalo Woman.

"I get the dogs," added Buffalo Calf as he pointed his finger first at his chest then in the reverse direction meaning he would return with them.

The Plains People could barely understand each other; nevertheless, communication was necessary for trade and the exchange of information. The Plains People estimated from thirty-one to thirty-seven tribes with one hundred fifty thousand to four hundred thousand people; therefore, a universal sign language was used before the Europeans came to America which was understood by all tribes. These hand movements were simple and logical. Each symbol either represented a word or a concept.

The travois was carefully constructed with a platform which was fastened to two poles.

"My dog carries a hundred pounds," gloated Buffalo Calf, "and more."

"Teepee heavy," reminded Buffalo Woman who did not need to be reminded of several tanned buffalo hides she had sewed together and laid over a form of poles. "Material heavy. Make teepees small for dogs for dray."

"Poles too light. Make teepee sag," complained Broken-Tooth-In-The-Middle.

"Make new teepee for the hunt," offered Buffalo Woman.

"Me bring home buffalo hides," added Uncle Buffalo Hide.

Buffalo Woman soaked the buffalo hides in the mud of the river until the hair loosened and could be scraped off easily by an elk rib scraper.

"Me peg out skins on ground," said Buffalo Woman.

"Pat flesh side up," instructed Buffalo Woman's sister.

Together, the sisters joined in scraping off the fat and fleshy parts with sheep scrappers made from elk bone.

"Me boil paste of the buffalo's brains and fat and bone grease," voiced another sister.

And together they spread the paste thickly over the skins. Then they let a day pass and washed the skins clean with warm water and hung them to dry. Finally, they rubbed and twisted and pulled each skin over a sharp edged beam.

"I help," added Buffalo Calf.

When it was all over, the skins were tanned leather, soft and white.

"I lay the skins," added Buffalo Woman.

She then proceeded to dip her fingers into red paint. Her sisters looked onward as she marked how they were to be cut. Together they cut them and sewed the pieces together into one big sheet. To sew they used sinew, a band of tough, fibrous tissue attaching a muscle to the backbone of the buffalo bone.

"I shred sinew," said Buffalo Calf, for he knew this was his job.

Instead of using needles, the women made holes in the skin with awls and pushed the sinew through the holes.

"Use sinew wet," said Buffalo Woman's sister. "When it dries, it never breaks."

After all the pieces were sewed together, Buffalo Woman and her sisters made a teepee in the form of a half moon.

"I make two smoke flaps at this edge," added Buffalo Woman.

Buffalo Calf and his helpers put up the pole frames and weighted it all around the bottom with stones, and they kept the smoke flaps in place with poles.

These are like the dampers in our chimney, thought Nelson Paige to himself.

They could be adjusted for any wind so that the smoke from the fire in the center of the teepee floor would rise straight up and go out at the top, instead of circling around inside.

Buffalo Woman and her sisters set out to decorate their clothing, bags, and baskets. Only certain women were trained in this art of decorating with quills.

"Need porcupine quills to decorate," said Buffalo Woman to her sisters. "This animal eats bark high in trees during winter, then shifts to plants on the ground in summer. Its quills are good defense but do no keep all animals away like us. Be careful of their tails. They swing their tails much farther, faster, and harder than you might expect."

With blanket in hand Buffalo Woman and her sisters were off to a hunt for a porcupine.

"Over there in the bush," alerted Buffalo Woman.

Buffalo Woman's sisters circled the porcupine while Buffalo Woman threw her blanket over the porcupine. The entrapment of the porcupine excited them and at the same time delivered ease of mind.

"Pull off blanket," instructed Buffalo Woman to her sisters.

As they removed the blanket, there were quills of every length. It was a perfect pluck. Different sizes of quills were needed for different types of embroidery.

"Dye quills different colors," further instructed Buffalo Woman.

This was followed by flattening the quills, and then they were sewed into a design. Eventually, the quills were replaced with beads because of the brightness of their color and the ability to work with them more easily.

The warrior and the hunters wore buckskin leggings and moccasins shimmering with porcupine quills. They carried clubs, tomahawks, knives, lances, and spears, as well as bows and great sheaves of arrows in quivers.

"We gather up dogs," said Buffalo Woman to the other women. Several hundred dogs were gathered.

Arf! Arf! Arf!

The village was permeated by the sound of the dogs were made ready for their journey.

Arf! Arf! Arf! "

I get the travois from storage place and tie to dogs," said Buffalo Calf. He went to the earth lodge to get the travois. Next came the gee-gaws and the knickknacks needed for the two to three months of wandering.

A...rrr...h! A...rrr...h! *A...rrr...h! A...rrr...h!*

A long, drawn out cry came from one of the dogsIt was summer, and a bushy, tail porcupine seemed to swish its tail out of the bush as it made various grunts, whines, and whistles.

"Smells like chicken soup," said Buffalo Woman's sister number one.

Then before her eyes was a large, nearly round rodent covered with quills. His dark brown to black body stood twenty-five inches long; twenty to thirty pounds in weight.

"Dogs never seem to learn to keep away from them," offered Buffalo Woman.

"Dog hurt!" added sister number two pregnant with child.

Immediately Buffalo Woman and her sisters began to care for their dog by pulling the quills out of his nose.

When the teepees and clothing were finished, three hundred people joined Buffalo Calf, Buffalo Woman, and her sisters for the big hunt. However, the hunt would not go immediately as had been planned.

"*Oh! Oh!*" sister number two moaned.

The excitement from trapping the porcupine was too much, and it hurried the birth of the child of sister number two. Children were warmly welcomed into the Plains People since very few of them lived after the first year of their life due to cholera, small pox, and measles epidemics; consequently, adjustments in the Plains People's plans were at hand. The journey would be interrupted by the child's birth and the naming ceremony.

Buffalo Woman pounded a strong stake into the ground for sister number two.

"Squat beside the stake and hold on with both hands," she instructed.

Holding its top with both hands the cramps of sister number two flushed through her body. When the child was born, the umbilical cord was given special attention. Buffalo Woman wrapped it in soft grass and oiled it with buffalo grease.

"Get puff ball," Buffalo Woman instructed sister number one.

Then she pulled the umbilical cord through the puff ball made from fungi and sprinkled it with its spores.

"I'll tie it to the baby," added sister number one.

"I'll tie the afterbirth high in the tree," followed Buffalo Woman.

After the child was four days old, it was time for it to he named but not before the "giveaway," the Sioux exhibition of generosity. First gifts were given to the very poor and powerful. Sister number two was given a feast, and her husband named the new baby Little-Man-Afraid-of-His-Journey for his most powerful vision—the trials ahead for a newborn in the life of a nomad.

Meanwhile, Buffalo Calf enumerated the items required for such a trip.

"Packs!"

"Bundles!"

"Teepees!"

"Sacks of cornmeal!"

Buffalo Woman added:

"Cooking pots!"

"Ladles!"

"Buffalo horn spoons!"

Buffalo Calf added in Chorus a second time.

"Fleshing knives!

"Knickknacks!"

"Let the dance begin," said Buffalo Calf.

The medicine man took from his medicinal pouch herbs needed to save the tribes people. He'd boil herbs such as sage over a brazier used to warm the tepee and gave it to them to drink. The entire tepee would be saturated with the odor of sage. Then he worked magic tricks to insure a safe journey and a safe return.

CHAPTER 11

Vision Quest

The medicine man or shaman was a holy person who had much power and knowledge. He healed the sick, interpreted dreams, visions, and other signs. He had special powers that are not normal or natural, so that he could do impossible things.

"Shaman decides when time to hunt," contributed Uncle Buffalo Hide. "He foretell future and pray to Spirits."

The shamans were thought to have close contact with the spirit world. They cast out evil spirits, brought good fortune to the tribe, and c ured diseases. Although the shaman's chief function was to summon good spirits, he sometimes performed black magic.

"Go on vision quest," Buffalo Hide said to Buffalo Calf.

"What is a vision quest?" quipped Buffalo Calf.

"Vision quest lasts one to four days. You fast and go to a quiet, lonely place," offered Buffalo Hide, "Time to explain further."

Buffalo Hide then began to map out a basic map for the spiritual journey.

"It is to seek out your own center," added Buffalo Hide.

The center that Uncle Buffalo Hide was talking about to Nelson Paige is to coincide to the center of the world where life originates.

"When the correspondence is reached, the bowels of the earth blaze up and dance in the air for a long time, giving the vision seeker light and warmth," explained Buffalo Hide. "If you help others, a space in your body opens to receive blessings. You will receive 'okahue.'"

"Okahue?" Nelson Paige asked. "What is okahue?"

"The five basic virtues: honor, justice, respect, dignity, and courage."

"I want to see the flame blaze in me. I want all of these," Buffalo Calf returned. "I want to go on a vision quest."

"Me too," said Nelson Paige.

Training for the vision quest to seek "okahue" was about to begin. When Buffalo Calf was taken to a shaman, upon his return to interpret his vision, the messenger of the quest often took the form of an animal. Sometimes young men were given a special name. A medicine bundle was prepared for Buffalo Calf with tokens to represent the guiding spirit.

"Put stones, skins, skull of mouse, wild turkey beak, braided grass, tobacco pipe, and a food bowl into rawhide pouch for you," said the shaman to Buffalo Calf.

Medicine bundles kept in rawhide pouches were collections of objects believed to have magical powers. The articles inside the bundles varied but usually included strangely shaped stones, the skins and skulls of animals, braided grass, a tobacco pipe, and a food bowl. Each item was a precious possession and represented a spiritual part of Buffalo Calf's life. They were believed to heal and protect him. With each year of age new items were added. Buffalo Calf knew when he passed on to the next world the bundle would be buried with him or passed on to a friend.

For the hunt, not only would Buffalo Calf's medicine bundle be opened, but the tribal bundle, too, would be opened. It was much larger and contained special objects that held meaning for the tribe. Not anyone was allowed to handle the tribal medicine bundle. It was opened on special occasions by certain members.

Having brush or timber piled up against the entrance as if to preserve, the contents closed some of the teepees. Others had huge pieces cut from their sides. In most of the tepees the fires were still burning. Nelson arrived at one, the interior of which was quite dark, the fire having almost died out. He procured a light fagot, and prepared to explore it; but not sooner had he entered the tepee the fagot failed him, leaving him in total darkness.

Nelson began feeling his way about the interior of the teepee. He had almost made the circuit when his hand came in contact with a human foot; at the same time a voice, unmistakably a member of the tribe and which evidently came from owner of the foot, convinced him that he was not alone. Nelson's next impression was that in their preparation for hasty flight, they had gone and left this one asleep. His next reaction, very naturally, related to himself. Nelson planned to interview its occupant but, unfortunately, would have to pass over or around the aforementioned foot and voice. Nelson feared that among the noble man's toiletry might be a tomahawk, scalping knife, a pistol, or possibly a war club. To avoid a questionable struggle for life, he crouched in silence.

Each moment spent in darkness of the tepee seemed like an age. He could hear a slight movement on the part of the unknown neighbor, which did not add to any comfort. Nelson, upon discovering the foot, drew his hunting knife from its scabbard and stood waiting the denouncement. Finally, directly below wrapped in a buffalo robe, lay the cause of his anxiety—an old, decrepit Indian of the Sioux tribe, who also had been deserted, owing to his infirmities and inability to travel with the tribe.

The other stay-at-homes had to tend the gardens and protect the village from outside invaders. Crowding upon the two earth lodges gave them a better view of their departing tribe. The hunters marched—and marched—and marched—and marched—and marched—and marched—and marched—and marched—and marched—and marched—and marched—and marched between the lodges

…through the pole gate of the fort wall

…across the yellow grass

…toward the setting sun.

Men shouted, women called, children scampered and squealed and got lost in the crowd. When they found their way back to their families, they were tied safely on their family's travois.

Wh…oo…f! Wh…oo…f! Wh…oo…f!

The dogs barked and howled and wagged their tails and bent forward in their harnesses to signal their readiness.

Swish! Swish! Swish!

The dragging poles of the travois left a small trail in the dust of the earth.

Buffalo Calf made a coughing sound as he fanned his outstretched hand in front of his face. Dust sprang into the warm air in an ever-rising cloud. This river of people was soon lost in the long grass and dust to the sight of those who were positioned on the tops of the lodges.

Wah! Wah! Wah!

The sounds of Buffalo Calf's baby brother could be heard as the big dog pulled him on the travois.

Clang! Clang! Clang!

The sounds of the family cooking pots making contact to each other seemed to be in competition with the screeching cries of the baby that permeated the air.

Ahead in the procession could be seen the curled tails of the dogs showing their eagerness to move ahead. Here and there a feather paused and nodded in midst of the dust. Momentarily, a brave paused to watch it until it landed on the ground. Behind Buffalo Calf stood other people and the panting dogs bearing the weight of their master's possessions.

CHAPTER 12

The Maelstrom

Through the dream catcher Nelson Paige was able to look back toward the stay-at-homes to see what was happening in the village.

"What's happening?" Nelson questioned himself as the dream catcher seemed to shake in his hand. "It must be a bad dream that was clogging the flow of images from passing through the webbing," he determined.

The stay-at-homes, left to tend the gardens and protect the village from outside invaders, were being attacked by another kind of invader unlike the marchers who had no idea of what they had left behind.

Crowded on the tops of the earth lodges came a sound like nothing heard before to their ears. The noise thermometer and other nearby wonders were brought alive by the rising temperature of the summer season. As the falling temperatures inhibited the vital processes of the insects, the rising temperatures were now stimulating them to sing.

Nelson remembered from his summer camp instructor two years ago telling him about how every nine degrees doubled insect consumption of oxygen, and everything that happens in their bodies speeds up correspondingly. Today was no exception.

When the braves felt something warm between their legs and crawling up their arms, they started making long, drawn out sounds of pain.

"Its crickets," cried out one of the braves, as they were running in every direction thrashing their arms in a circular motion to protect their faces and rid their food and clothing of their presence. This was only postponing the inevitable.

They watched with trepidation as a cloud of crickets began to attack. The crickets had become very active because of the oxygen increase and were jumping everywhere and invading any food that was left for their taking.Not even one brave feigned to be calm. They were under *attack*. Their minds worked frantically to thwart them off.

Nelson automatically knew the temperature. To tell the correct temperature all you have to do is watch the insects in your backyard and listen to the sounds. If you can't hear any insect sounds at all, this means that the temperature is below forty degrees; all insects are silent when it's that chilly. If you can hear some insect sounds but can't see any ants, it's a sure sign that the mercury stands somewhere between forty and forty-four degrees; ants remain in their nests until the temperature gets up to forty-four degrees.

But Nelson knew the most accurate way to tell temperature—more accurate certainly than the average thermometer, whose mercury column nearly always lags behind the fact—was the common chirp of the cricket.

"Where's my watch, the one with the second hand?" Nelson asked himself. Then he began to count for fourteen seconds. "One second…Two seconds…Three seconds…Four seconds…Five seconds…Six seconds…Seven seconds…Eight seconds…Nine seconds…Ten seconds…Eleven seconds…Twelve seconds…Thirteen seconds…Fourteen seconds…" and then he added the number forty to his count. "And that's it. That's the exact temperature in degrees Fahrenheit!" he yelled. He looked around to make sure that no one heard him.

Of course, he knew that the insect activity of the cricket wouldn't increase indefinitely with the rising temperatures. They too had hearts like everyone else, and eventually the exertion beyond their beating heart would be too exhausting. He knew that they would stop pestering the stay-at-homes at about ninety degrees, and at 105 degrees the world would be silent again—all would be taking a well-earned siesta.

Most of all, Nelson Paige remembered being fascinated most by the chirping sounds of the cricket besides its unusual talent to tell the temperature. Today was no exception for them to demonstrate this talent to the stay-at-homes. The sounds that they made were the result of a built-in fiddle system, carried by the male of the species. Nelson Paige could visualize the male rubbing the leading edge of each wing, which has a rough surface like that of a file, on its underside. In the same place, but on top of the wing, is a scraper. They rubbed the two together like a bow on a violin.

"You can hear the cricket serenade," murmured Nelson Paige to himself.

This was how the male cricket attracted the female cricket; however, this wasn't always the case. Sometimes a male cricket would respond to the mating call. This would result in a fight, during which there was a chewing off of antennae, limbs, and heads.

"Thank goodness! No ears to bite off," laughed Nelson Paige.

"Why? Because crickets don't have ears. They hear each other through holes in their forelegs."

Another wonder of the cricket is their remarkable appetite. They were living up to this by eating anything they could get their ant like mandible into in the village: meat, seeds, grass, leaves, leather, old and new clothing—even another cricket if they can't get meat any other way. Nelson Paige knew from experience, that whatever they wanted to eat, they grabbed with their powerful forelegs and started munching.

The voracious appetite of the cricket was witnessed as they attacked the village. Eating all the things that the stay-at-homes wanted for themselves caused a confrontation between the insects and them. It was the time of year when the open fields and grassy plains were quite crowded with crickets, walking sticks, green katydids, and grasshoppers; however, never before did they attack the stay-at-homes.

Nelson Paige waited for nightfall. Meanwhile, he observed the chaos created by the crickets and listened to their music.

"Stridulation! Stridulation! *Yes, that's what their music is called*," he thought, as he remembered from his summer camp instructor.

Upon returning from camp two years previous, Nelson Paige recalled how he kept one for a pet. With their music and their uninhibited table manners, they made a good pet for him. Placing it in a glass jar, he filled the bottom with a little earth and punched plenty of small holes in the top for air. Each day he made sure he fed him a well-balanced diet, as omnivorous as his own: meat scraps from the table, fresh vegetable fragments, and fresh cereal grains. Then he took a shallow bottle top and made a watering trough for them.

It was like having his own science lab in his room. Being one of the most primitive orders of the insect world, he soon discovered that they reached maturity by way of incomplete metamorphosis; that is without going through larval and pupal stages like the butterfly he had in another jar. After the eggs hatched, the young simply went through a series of molts. But to Nelson's surprise, each time they molted they were bigger, and their appearance had changed only slightly, and the adult form didn't really look too different from the newly hatched youngster; both of them looked like they came from the same family member.

At first, Nelson Paige was sure the stay-at-homes were attacked by locusts or grasshoppers. To his relief he soon discovered that were "cold-blooded" crickets had attacked them. Do not be misled by the term; it can be misleading. Actually it means that their body temperature rises and falls with the temperature of the air around them. At any rate, nightfall had come and the temperature was dropping quickly. A drop of just a few degrees made life for the stay-at-homes more agreeable. The drop in temperature caused the crickets to become dormant and escape back to their habitats.

"Whew!" Nelson Paige breathed with a sigh of relief.

The crickets' fury was nothing like the locust or grasshoppers that buzzed and destroyed crops and grass. They could have destroyed the entire stay-at-home people's village.

"Oh look!" said Nelson, as the images from the dream catcher seemed to flow through the web once again with clarity.

CHAPTER 13

May the Wind Always Be At Your Back

"We march in a straight line," said Buffalo Hide. "Scout go ahead to look for game and water."

"We lead the procession," came the voice of one of the four old chiefs, the wisest of the band.

The wise old chiefs carried the sacred pipes and medicine bundles of the tribe to ward off evil.

"They say where camps will be and when to start the hunt," added Buffalo Hide.

After the wise old chiefs came the women and children with the dogs—a number of them attached by a cord shaped into a long, thin line.

"Every fourth one have travois," informed Buffalo Hide. "Other three be back-ups to bring meat back after the hunt."

Buffalo Woman and her sisters kept close together. All the tribesmen wished for a good hunt. To replenish their meat supply the women and children were aware of the teamwork required.

"Hunt to give much meat to our tribe," said Buffalo Woman to her sisters.

At the rear on both sides of the baggage train were warriors.

"Warriors heavily armed to protect us," Buffalo Woman assured her sisters. "Warriors protect us."

On each side of the baggage train the warriors protected the women and children. Contrary to the tribes' fears, according to scouts there were no enemies in their territory this hunting season.

The procession of the tribes' people started late; therefore, not much territory was covered. Then came the directive all the tribes' people were waiting for that day.

"We camp now!" articulated Number One Chief.

It was an automatic cue for the dogs. The ones with the loads dropped to the ground.

Huh! Huh! Huh!

Their exertion caused them to breathe short, labored gasps. Panting as they lay in the grass caused a rasping need for air as they breathed in unison. It created a grating voice.

"Take harnesses off dogs," instructed Buffalo Woman to her sisters.

"Unlash the baggage from the travois poles," added one of Buffalo Woman's sisters with her burnt-sugar-colored eyes.

The work between Buffalo Woman and her sisters created a quiet bond among them. Something good for all of them blossomed. They gained companionship and teamwork.

"What happy dogs they are now," responded Buffalo Woman, as they rolled in the grass. There before their very eyes were the dogs lengthening, widening, and extending their legs to release the strain to their muscles. Some extended their limbs further. In so doing the muscles became more tightened and taunt. Then this was followed by rapid onward movement toward the water. At first, as they took in the water with their tongues, the soft liquid sounds could be heard. The sound became louder and louder as they greedily competed for the disappearing water.

"Time to put up willow poles," instructed Number *Two* Chief.

The women began to build supports with willow poles on the slope that was higher than the surrounding country.

"Kree-kree re-e-e-e!" came crying sounds like a squealing pig. Temporarily it interrupted their work. It was a Krider Red-tailed hawk, sitting itself on a willow pole, a common habit of its kind. Then it swooped down to catch a field mouse with its sharply curved bill. It picked up a field mouse with it claws, and because of the way its legs are jointed, they bound tightly around the rodent as it squirmed in an attempt to free itself from its demise. Then the hawk was off in flight after flying about with outspread wings over the field, as if it were doing a victory lap in the air.

Buffalo Woman took upon herself to make sure the legends of the tribe were passed on to other members of the tribe, and the legend about the hawk was given birth.

> *Once there was a very bad brave, who never liked to do a good deed or say a pleasant word, and one night an ugly, old witch ran after him because he was teasing her. The brave started to run as fast as he could run, but the witch could run faster and gained on him. The harder the brave ran, the faster the witch ran. She had almost reached him when the brave began to cry for help, and suddenly he felt himself changed into a hawk. In the new form he escaped from the enraged woman.*

Gradually, they returned to developing and increasing the stages of the tripods of willow. Each reached skyward in harmony. It was a mysterious quality of enchantment to see all the teepees on the high country.

Magic! Magic! Magic! Magic! The spectacle before them in the grass was pure magic.

"We are the masters of our fate," agreed Chief Number One, Chief Number Two, Chief Number Three, and Chief Number Four. Buffalo Woman and her sisters, Buffalo Calf, and Uncle Buffalo Hide joined in agreement to the task completed.

The teepees formed a circle two rows deep. Other poles were leaned against each other forming a point. These pointed frames seemed to sprout up like young plants, giving off shoots or buds in a circular fashion. Finally, the flapping teepee covers came to finish their symmetrical creations. The exact correspondence of form and configuration on opposite sides of the axis gave the teepee balance or harmonious proportions. This symmetry was transferred to their arrangement into a circle for the entire tribe.

"Go find rocks!" instructed Chief Number Three to Buffalo Calf. Racing to the river-bank went Buffalo Calf and his friends in search of the perfect sized rocks.

"Here's one," someone called out to the others as he lifted in the air a round, water-worn boulder from the clay. "Good to stop the wind from blowing the tepee over in the winter."

"Here's another!" came another voice.

"Ouch!" still another offered, as he stubbed his foot on one jetting from the water. He soon discovered that it wasn't the rock that caused pain to his foot but rather old buffalo skulls and bones. It was here that they found the stones that they needed. The stones were the size of a soccer ball, the perfect size to lie upon the bison hides that formed the cone shape of the teepees with an opening at the top and an opening that faced eastward to the rising sun.

"We make thongs," said Buffalo Calf. Thongs were the invention created out of necessity to transport the stones over the slippery grass.

"Bring dogs," instructed Buffalo Woman, "to attach the thong piled with stones to the dogs."

The strain on their muscles was evident as they drug the hides over the morning dew, the moisture that had condensed from the air in small drops upon the cool surfaces during the evening. Periodically, a foot slid causing a slip in their forward motion. Suddenly, for that moment in space and time, the dogs were checked by the pure and innocent dew of the morning.

Buffalo Woman and the women looked back at their creations that were so easy to set up and take down. It was warm in the winter and cool in summer and waterproof.

Two longer poles were attached to the smoke-flaps at the top of the tepee.

"Flaps like chimney," thought Nelson Paige.

"We open to let smoke escape," contributed Buffalo Woman. "In hot weather we roll up cover from bottom to let air circulate. Sometimes use pegs instead of stones and pound into the ground around bottom of tepee covering.

The average tepee was five meters or sixteen feet in diameter. Depending on its size, it took eight to twenty hides sewn together with sinew to make the teepee cover.

"Tepee sleep five to seven people," offered Buffalo Woman.

The interior of the tepee was dimly lighted by the decaying embers of a small fire built in the centre. All around were usual adornments and articles, which constitute the household items of Uncle Buffalo Hide and his extended family.

The tepee was lined with bear, bison, or deer skin in the winter. There was very little furniture inside. Beds made from bison skins were placed against the outside walls. Elk-Woman and the women tied willows together with cords for backrests, making it more comfortable to sit. Fur-lined skins covered the floor.

"Keep food, clothing, tools in buffalo-hide pouches," said Buffalo Woman.

"Hang bags from poles or set against walls inside the tepee," instructed Buffalo Woman, as a deer mouse, all one ounce of it, ran across the floor. A gray to reddish-brown three to four inches long body with a white belly and very long tail of two to five inches between its legs as it took a double take at what was waiting for its next meal before it motored behind the bags.

Though the deer mouse with its big sparkling eyes is a common mouse, it thrives on seeds, nuts, fruits, insects, and fungi. It wasn't unusual to see one coming out of an old bird's nest. Buffalo Woman knew, despite its small size and quickness, the small creature was a problem because many predators fed on them. The moment they were born, they were the prey of other animals that could and would interrupt their lifestyle.

Buffalo robes were spread like carpets over the floor; head mats, used to recline upon, were arranged as if for the comfort of their owners; parfleches, a sort of Native American box, with their contents apparently undisturbed, were found carefully stowed away under the edges or border of the tepee. These, with the doormats, paint-bags, rawhide ropes, and other equipment, were left as if the owners had been absent for a period.

To complete the picture of the tepee, over the fire hung a camp kettle, in which in which by the means of the dim light of the fire, we could see what had been intended for the supper of the late occupants of the tepee. Savory odors arose from the dark recesses of the mysterious kettle. Buffalo Calf cast himself about the tepee looking for some instrument to aid him in his pursuit of knowledge of what was cooking. He found a horn spoon, with which he began his investigation of the contents, finally succeeding in getting possession of a fragment that might have been the half of a duck, or rabbit, judging from its size.

"Ah!" said Buffalo Calf in his most complacent manner, "Here is the opportunity I have been awaiting."

He often desired to test and taste his mother's cooking in the process of its stewing.

"What do you suppose this is?" holding up the dripping morsel.

Unable to obtain the desired information, Buffalo Calf, whose naturally good appetite had been sensibly sharpened, set to with a will and ate heartily of the mysterious contents of the kettle.

"What can this be?" Buffalo Calf inquired again.

He was only satisfied on one point—it was delicious—a dish fit for a king. Just then Uncle Buffalo Hide entered the tepee. To him Buffalo Calf appealed for information since he had maturity and experience and years spent with the tribes. Fishing out a huge piece and attacking it with the voracity of a hungry wolf, he was not long in determining what Buffalo Calf had supped so heartily upon. His first words settled the mystery:

"Why, this is dog!"

I will not attempt to repeat the few but emphatic words uttered by Buffalo Calf as he rushed from the tepee. Fortunately, with the help of Buffalo Woman, the mood of the tepee was changed to a more upbeat note.

"We decorate tepee with painting, "said Buffalo Woman to her sisters.

"Make animals, stars, and other objects," added sister number three of Buffalo Woman.

"I take care of Little-Man-Afraid-Of-His-Journey," offered sister number two.

CHAPTER 14

Connected to Nature

For the Plains People bison was a spiritual animal because it provided them with the staples of daily life—food, clothing, shelter, and tools. When their supply grew low, the tribes people prayed to Mother Earth to awaken the spirits to lead them to where the bison roamed or camped.

The Buffalo Dance was intended to bring the spirit of the buffalo closer to the tribal hunting grounds. Dancers wearing buffalo skins imitated the animals' movements in order to attract them for meat to eat, hides to make teepees, clothing and bone to make tools.

The bear for the Plains People was the ears of the forest. All the bear wanted was respect and not to be aggravated. However, if a human or another threat perpetrated their territory, action would be taken. The bear only sought to defend itself. Being a large, very strong mammal with a heavy, thickly furred body and short tail, it delivered a message to all evildoers. To the attacker the bear seemed larger than life itself. He was like a gruff, clumsy person.

The great horned owl, king of the owls, was a strange legend; nevertheless, Buffalo Woman loved to share the story over and over with her sisters.

There once was a widow who had only one daughter, and the mother often told the girl, "You must be married and then there will be a man to go hunting."

One day a man came courting the daughter, and he asked her, "Will you marry me?" "I can only marry a man who will work," replied the girl. "I am just that kind of man," said the man, so the mother said that the couple might be married.

One day, the mother gave the man a hoe and told him, "Go and hoe the corn. When breakfast is ready I will call you."

When she went to call him, she found that he had hoed only a very small piece of ground, and she wondered what he had been doing. In a nearby thicket she heard something that sounded like "You awake? Me too!"

"Whoo!"

"Whoo-whoo-whoo!"

"Who!"

"Who!"

The man did not come back until evening and the mother asked him where he had been all day.

"Hard at work," he responded, but when the mother said she could not find him when she had come to call him, he looked rather startled and replied, "I was out cutting sticks with which to mark the fields."

Early the next morning the man left with the hoe, and again the mother went out to call him. But she found the hoe lying in the field and the man sitting in a thicket trying to mock a little owl. That night when the man camehome, the mother was so angry she drove him from the house and said that he should be changed into a great horned owl.

The owl would give a piercing and weird scream. Usually at the end of the day's labors the owl would perch on a limb and give a loud, deep-toned cry, which would start out with a scream like that of a woman in great agony and end with a wild call.

"Who-hoo-hoo!"

"Who-hoo-hoo!"

Hearing the owl's hoot would warn the tribes' people about death or about something gloomy about to happen.

Before marriage a young woman was kept carefully away from men, but courtship still took place by playing a flute, flashing a mirror outside the girl's tepee to gain attention, or approaching her when she went for water. Men married about thirty years of age after they'd proven themselves warriors.

Marriages were between one man and one woman, but marriages between one man and up to four or vie women wasn't uncommon. Usually, additional wives were sisters to the first wife. Divorce was easy. A woman living in her husband's lodge simply returned to her mother's lodge, and men living with his wife's people went back to his mother's lodge.

Unlike the owl in the Plains stories and legends, the eagle was referred to as the thunderbird associating it with lightening.

"Eagle majestic!" said Buffalo Woman.

"Eagle fierce and focused!" exclaimed sister number one.

"Eagle wait and watch before it falls on its prey.

"Eagle independent!" added sister number two.

"Eagle proud and solitary!" followed sister number three.

The eagle was revered for its great powers of vision. For the Plains People the eagle had great powers of vision, soared to great heights, and had great strength and courage. Black-tipped eagle feathers were sought after because they were priceless possessions. Eagle feathers were used for ceremonies; also, to receive an eagle feather as a reward signaled you out as a brave person. Wing bones of the eagle were made into whistles. The eagles' talons look like crooked hands but are used to clasp the rugged rock upon which he lands. Often displayed around the tribesmen's necks were talons that were good luck charms.

CHAPTER 15

Rough It

The women set up the teepees in less than an hour, and took them down in a matter of minutes—a record time for anyone who has ever camped in open nature. The ends of two of the long poles were tied to a dog. The other ends were dragged on the ground forming a travois in an A-shape.

The camp was not a magical accident; however, the chiefs, all four of them, with their families were positioned in the immediate center of the camp. Then came the circle-within-a-circle. The smoke flap was essential to relieve the smoke from the fire pits since fire making was an act among them on a daily basis.

Making a fire took on as many different forms as there were different people. In some tribes a sacred fire was created by a circle of warriors or chiefs who took turns spinning a round stick between their palms, back and forth. The lower end of the stick was shaved to a point and drilled into a shallow pit in a small board on the ground. Friction between the stick and the board produced a brown powder and then wisps of smoke. When the powder turned jet black and smoked in little clouds, the stick was removed and the powder fanned. Then a red coal appeared, no larger than a sparrow's eye. Fine grass or small bark tinders were placed on top and blown into a flame. This was the slowest of the methods and would be reserved for *sacred* fires.

A method requiring less energy was to wind once about the stick, a thong, of which the ends were fastened to the tips of a bent stick. The top of the stick was held steady against a stone grip, and the bent stick was sawed back and forth. The thong spun the drill much faster than human hands can do it. Thus, a coal was created in a half minute or less.

Cooking fires were built outside the teepees. First a circle of grass was burned away so that there was no danger of starting a prairie fire. In the center of the burned patch the fire was laid. Again, a byproduct of the buffalo was utilized.

"Buffalo chips!" said Buffalo Woman, "used for fuel."

The sun-dried cakes were scattered in the deep trails and along the river bottoms. The gray color and the crusty texture of the droppings made them easy to locate for the fuel hunters.

Buffalo Woman never doubted the gifts of the buffalo, nor did the tribes people. The buffalo was their brother. As Buffalo Woman's son drug a hide filled with chips, the gifts the buffalo provided ran across her mind. Foremost, they provided the teepee followed close behind was food and sleeping robes. Next were tools and weapon points provided by the bones of the skeleton. Because of their texture the horns were used for bows. The hoofs were cooked into glue. The buffalo carried his own tanning materials for his hide, his own sewing thread and bone awls. Of course, the grass the buffalo ate packed lightly in his droppings and dried into light firm chips to make the finest fuel.

One of the camps pitched on the banks of a small stream, coincidentally, had been named Beaver Creek. Surely this was an opportunity to kill a few beavers, as they were very numerous all along this stream, which had derived its name from the fact. The numerous stumps and fallen trees, as well as the beaver dams, attested to its name. We waited until sundown before taking our stations on the bank, not far above the site of the camp as at that time the beaver would be out and on shore.

A small party proceeded to place themselves on the ground selected, where they distributed singly at stations along the stream and quietly awaited the appearance of the beaver. They waited at their station ready to fire at the first beaver, which should offer itself as a sacrifice. Until the sun disappeared and darkness had begun to spread its heavy mantle over everything, no living thing had thus far been disturbed. Uncle Buffalo Hide's station was on the immediate bank of the stream, on a path that had evidently been made by wild animals of some kind. The bank rose above me to a distance of nearly twenty feet. Buffalo Hide was just on the point of leaving his station and giving up all hope of getting a shot, when he heard something rustle in the long grass a few yards down stream.

Cocking his rifle, Buffalo Hide stood ready to deliver its contents into the approaching animal, which he presumed would be a beaver as soon as it should emerge from the tall grass. For a minute, which became a year, Buffalo Hide was superstitious and then fearful.

"Evil is tangible thing—with wave lengths. Evil thing speak and give off vibrations like now," he muttered to himself silently.

It had not made its appearance in the path in which he stood until within a few feet of him, when, to his surprise, he beheld, instead of a beaver, an immense wildcat. It was difficult to say who was more surprised, Buffalo Hide or the wildcat.

"Maybe! But sometimes wildcat have an extra sense that tells them that they are in danger," suggested Buffalo Hide.

Which of them should retain the right of way on shore, the path being too narrow to admit to their passing each other? Without delaying long to think, Buffalo Hide took a hasty aim and fired. The next moment a splash was heard. It was a relief to Buffalo Hide. Buffalo Hide had either wounded or killed the wildcat, and its body was being carried down in the darkness with the current. The dogs, which were soon attracted from the camp by Buffalo Hide's shot, were unable to find the trail on either bank.

The sensuous drowsiness of night was upon Buffalo Hide.

"*It's dark,*" he thought. "*I could sleep without closing eyes.*" The curtain of night was on Buffalo Hide's eyelids.

CHAPTER 16

Telegraphing

So then did the stay-at-homes never hear again from the wanderers? No, they developed a simple mode of telegraphing. And this is exactly what they did the night before the hunt. They signaled its beginnings. It was wonderful to what a state of perfection telegraphing was developed. Scattered over a great portion of the plains were isolated hills, or as they are usually termed "buttes," which can be seen from a distance of more than fifty miles. These peaks are selected as the telegraphic stations. By varying the columns of smoke different meanings were conveyed by the messages. The most simple as well as most easily varied mode and resembling somewhat the ordinary alphabet employed in the magnetic telegraph, is arranged by building a small fire, which is not allowed to blaze; then, by placing a armful of partially green grass or weeds over the fire, as if to smother it, a dense, white smoke is created, which will ordinarily ascend in a continuous vertical column for hundreds of feet. The column of smoke is used for telegraphing. This is like sending a text message on a cell phone. The alphabet, so far as it goes, was almost identical, consisting as it does of long lines and short lines or dots.

But how was it formed? The answer is by the simplest methods. Having his current of smoke established, a blanket is taken and spread over a small pile of weeds or grass from which the column of smoke takes its source, and properly controlling the edges and corners of the blankets, he confines the smoke and is in this way able to retain it for several moments. By rapidly displacing the blanket, the operator is able to cause a dense volume of smoke to rise, the length or shortness of which, as well as the number and frequency of the columns, he can regulate perfectly, simply by the proper use of the blanket. For the transmission of brief messages previously determined upon, no simpler method could be adopted.

As soon as the lookout near the village discerned the location of the hunting party, the intelligence is at once published to the stay-at-homes by the stentorian tones of the village crier, the duties of which office are usually performed by some deposed chief. Upon the wanderers return to the village, runners mounted upon fleet ponies are at once dispatched to meet the returning villagers and gather the particulars of the hunt—whether successful or otherwise, whether laden with buffalo meat or empty handed. These are questions that are speedily solved, when the wanderers hasten back to the village and announce the result, whereupon the occupants of the entire village, old and young, sally forth to meet the returning hunters. If the latter have been successful and no lives have been lost, they become the recipient of all the triumph a people are capable of heaping upon them.

Now sometimes the wanders came up against war parties. The same telegraphing system was used; however, the questions were different. The runners asked:

"Have they brought any prisoners and captured horses? And are your numbers unbroken or do their losses exceed their gains?' These and other questions are speedily solved.

They advanced toward the village painted and dressed in full war costumes, singing their war songs, discharging their firearms, and uttering ever and anon the war whoop peculiar to their tribe. Added to this, every person in the village capable of uttering a sound joins in the general rejoicing, and for a time the entire population is wild with excitement. If, however, instead of returning in triumph, the war party has met with disaster and suffered the loss of one or more warriors, the scene witnessed upon their arrival at the village is as boisterous as the other, but even more horrible. The party is met as before by all the inhabitants of the village but in a widely different manner; instead of shouts and songs of victory that greet the successful hunters, only screams and wails of an afflicted people are heard.

The war paint and the bright colors give way to a deep black which all the mourners and friends of the fallen warriors besmeared their faces. The members of the immediate family began slashing and sacrificing their faces, arms, and bodies with knives. Then cries were heard of the most piercing and horrible sound. A not infrequent mode of disfiguring themselves, and one which Buffalo Calf had seen, was for the mourner, particularly if the one mourned was a wife or husband, was to cut off the first joint of the little finger. This, of course, is done without the slightest regard for the rules of surgery, of which Buffalo Calf was ignorant. The operation is simply performed by taking a knife, often of questionable sharpness, and cutting through the flesh and first joint of the little finger, leaving no "flap" of flesh to cover the exposed bone. As a result, in healing, the flesh withdraws from the mutilated portion of the finger and usually leaves nearly an inch of bone exposed, presenting, of course, a most revolting appearance.

At any rate, the signal was telegraphed and the stay-at-home people were informed.

CHAPTER 17

Let's Go Hunting!

The last meal to be eaten the evening before the hunt was boiled jerky meat cooked quickly. By the time it was eaten, the sun was well on its way to bed into the western horizon. This signaled to the warrior sentries to go to their posts about the teepee circle.

"Everyone lay down on your robes," instructed Buffalo Hide.

"Can't sleep." Buffalo Calf was so excited his eyelids would not close.

Thump! Thump! Thump! Thump!

The horny sheath covering of the buffalo hoofs thundered as they traversed the earth. Or was it only thousand upon thousands of crickets singing, making shrill chirping sounds? Carefully, Buffalo Hide placed his ear to the earth to validate the sounds.

"The Great Hunt has dawned," roared Uncle Buffalo Hide.

He closed his eyes—just for a minute it seemed—but when he opened them again, the first faint light of the early morning was in a cloud of gray.

"Time to break camp!" hollered chief number four after breakfast was completed.

Whoof! Whoof! Whoof!

All the sounds seemed to intermingle from the dogs to the small children wailing in a high-pitched sound to the muffled sound produced by poles clattering downward to the ground.

Before Buffalo Calf realized what all the tumult was about, all the teepees and poles were placed into orderly piles, only achieved through ingenuity and skill. This was done right before Buffalo Calf's eyes not sure what it was all about.

"What's happening? What's all the excitement about?" inquired Buffalo Calf.

"Chiefs decided to leave now to make twenty-five miles before next sunset," explained Buffalo Woman. "Go straight west."

When the new day sun was nodding at the moving line of tribes people, they were already well on their way. Looking backward in their tracks, they viewed nothing except patches of burned grass and rings of teepee stones.

The plains looked like a road map with game trails going in every direction; of course, these were created by buffalo. These trails were as wide as they were deep and measured up to two feet. Porous, chalky, white skeleton buffalo bones were scattered here and there on the trails. It was either a long winter or an attack by gray wolves that left the buffalo stopped in their tracks. There they died mercilessly only to fulfill the cycle of life.

"There are many buffalo before us all the time. Why not shoot with arrows?" inquired Buffalo Calf.

"Too many—cause big problem," said Chief Number Four wearing a wolf's tail representing esteemed acts of warfare.

"If one buffalo see a hunter, he alerts the other buffalo," said Chief Number Two wearing white weasel fur.

"Stampede," added another Chief Number One in his ermine fur.

"Need large dog to hunt buffalo," added Chief Number Four.

"Run forty miles and not be able to hunt," added Chief Number One.

"But we have to do everything on foot," added Chief Number Four.

"We band together to catch buffalo," continued Chief Number Three as a solution.

"Dress in skins of wolves to stalk buffalo in tall grass," said Chief. Number Two.

However, the buffalo could care less about the wolves. It was only when their calves were attacked that the buffalo became defensive.

"We get close, within bowshot distance," said Chief Number Three dressed in his feather headdress.

Each feather represented a coup or a kill. The painting, notching, or positioning of the feathers gave further details of the military action.

"No, have to take great herd all at once, or we not eat all winter," said Chief Number One.

"And how is this great herd to be taken?" questioned Buffalo Calf.

"Be patient, and you will see," returned Chief Number Four, leaving Buffalo Calf to wander and think as he walked along in the grass path next to the dogs.

CHAPTER 18

The Waterspout

Shortly thereafter the trail had changed by the tribe people. It now extended sharply due North.

"Time to make a snare," whooped Buffalo Calf.

"Time to make dead fall," intervened Chief Number One.

"Ah," responded Buffalo Hide. "We are going to the big bluff. I haven't been there for several seasons."

"Why we go there?" inquired Buffalo Woman.

"There's a good buffalo trap there," added Buffalo Hide.

There was only silence from Uncle Buffalo Hide and Buffalo Calf as they followed their way along the winding shore of the river.

We camp here for the night," instructed Buffalo Hide.

Buffalo Hide confidently expected to spend a quiet night by the river, and at its termination planned to proceed onward with the tribes march. A few hours into the evening, a heavy rain set in. The immediate effect of the noticeable shower was nothing to be concerned over. However, the heaviest downpour occurred far above the point where the tribe camped. There, the rain poured down in the manner resembling that of a rainspout on a house during a powerful downpour. It was in the nighttime, after the entire camp, except for the scouts, had retired and fallen asleep. The stream ebbed, overcharged by the rushing volumes from above. It soon became transformed from a mild and murmuring brook into an irresistible, turbulent torrent of water.

Swish! Swish! Swish!

So sudden and unexpected had been the rise, that before the alarm could be given, thirty-six feet, which had separated the surface of the water began now sweeping over the entire plain. After overflowing the natural banks of the creek, the first new channel ran in such a manner as to surround the tents occupied by the tribe as well as that occupied by the chiefs. The tribes people hastened to the bluff to escape being swept down before the huge torrent that with each instant became more fearful.

To add to the embarrassment of the situation, the blackest darkness prevailed, only relieved at times by vivid gleams of lightning. At the same time a deep sullen roar of the torrent increased each moment in depth and volume and was drowned at intervals by the fierce and more deafening uproar of the thunder.

When Buffalo Woman awakened by the storm, she discovered a new channel surrounded her tent. All efforts to reach the main camp would prove unavailing. She had with her at this time only her sisters. They did not even know the fate of the other portion of the camp. In the midst of this fearful scene, they heard the loud sounds showering shock near their tent. The cries came from people being carried from their camp in the darkness by the rising current.

"No assistance can reach them," cried Buffalo Woman in despair for their existence.

"It doubtful they will be saved even if found in the daylight," bemoaned Buffalo Woman's sister.

The people swam doggedly in order to save themselves. Slow, deliberate strokes were taken to conserve their energy. For a seemingly long time, what seemed like one hundred strokes, they fought the river. There were four in all. Desperately, one of them stuck out with strong strokes trying to get out of a tight situation. As he was being swept by a tent, through accident no doubt, he grabbed the branch of a huge tree that leaned precariously on a small living one. But he was not quick enough, the dead tree crashed down and struck one of them a blow on his shoulders as it fell.

Help! Help! Help!

These were the cries coming from the voices of the gripping hearts. And then there continued a desperate, hopeless flight that carried the remaining three on for some distance. It was from him that the cries of distress principally came. He could be seen by Buffalo Woman and her sisters, this unfortunate man clinging, as it were, between life and death. With commendable presence of mind, Buffalo Woman and her sisters came to the rescue.

Get rope! Quick!

A rope was obtained, and after a few failures, one end was thrown to the unfortunate man, and by the united strength of Buffalo Woman and her sisters he was pulled to shore, and, for the time being at least, his life was saved. His three less fortunate companions were drowned.

Buffalo Hide and Buffalo Calf, with a view of rescuing Buffalo Woman and her sisters, had succeeded in making their way across the new channel made by the torrent to the knoll, but when attempting to return to the mainland, they found the current too deep and swift for them to succeed. They were compelled then to await their fate. The water continued to rise until the entire valley from the natural channel to the first bluff, a distance of a quarter of a mile, was covered by an unaffordable river. The only point still free from water was the little knoll, which had been selected so fortunately by the tribe. But the rise of the water continued until it finally reached the edge of the tent. At that rate, the tents themselves must soon be swept away.

When the water finally approached close to the tent, Buffalo Woman marked the progress from time to time by placing small stakes at the waterline. How anxiously the gradual rise of the torrent must have been watched. At last, when all hope seemed almost exhausted, the waters were stayed in progress, and soon, to the great joy of the party besieged, began to recede. It was still dark, but so rapidly did the volume of water diminish—as rapidly as it had accumulated—that a few hours after daylight a safe passage was created to the mainland.

With the exception of three lives, no more lives were lost, although narrow escapes were made.

In the morning, daylight showed the camp a mud-filled field with their belongings strewn everywhere and tribes people torn from all sides. After refreshing themselves, what remained was to say adieu to those who were to remain behind. From our campsite we could see a knoll upon which a platform was erected, which resembled somewhat of a hunting signal station. Curious as to what its purpose was, Nelson Paige was determined to visit it.

Taking with him Buffalo Calf, he soon reached the point and discovered that the object of his curiosity and surprise was a Native American grave. The body, instead of being consigned to Mother Earth, was placed on top of the platform. It was constructed of saplings and was about twenty feet in height. This was the mode of disposing of the body after death. When the flesh was decayed, they buried the bleached bones—except for the skulls, which they arranged in a sacred circle.

"When the body is done with this world, the spirit of the deceased is transferred to the 'happy hunting ground,'" offered Buffalo Calf. "Here he will be permitted to engage in the same pleasures and pursuits that he preferred on earth."

It was felt essential that after death the departed must be supplied with the same equipment and ornaments considered necessary while in the flesh. Boys were expected to follow in the footsteps of great warriors of their tribe. In compliance to the people's beliefs a complete outfit, depending in extent upon the rank of importance of the deceased, was prepared, and surrendered with the body to the final resting place. The body found on this occasion must have been that of a son of some important chief.

"See not full-grown but has all the arms and adornments owned by a warrior," pointed out Buffalo Calf.

Next to the warrior was a bow and quiver full of steel pointed arrows, the tomahawk and scalping knife, and a red clay pipe with a small bag full of tobacco. In order that the departed spirit should not be wholly dependent on friends after his arrival at the happy hunting ground, he had been supplied with provisions consisting of small parcels containing food. Weapons of modern structure had also been furnished him, a revolver and a rifle with powder and ball ammunition for each, and a saddle, bridle, and lariat for his pony. Added to this wearing apparel were paints for his face in case he needed them. A handsome buckskin scalping pocket, lavishly ornamented with beads completed the outfit. Not to frighten, a white woman's scalp was considered as a necessary accompaniment, a letter of introduction to the dusky warriors and chieftains who had gone before. Provisions for mounting the horse to heaven on earth were taken. To accomplish this, the dead party's favorite pony was led beneath the platform on which the body of the warrior was placed at rest, and there strangled to death.

The Sioux engaged in the practice of scalping. It was believed it came from the French whey they paid a bounty for scalps during the French and Indian Wars. It was a belief of the Natives that hair was akin to the spirit and life everlasting. Consequently, when a comrade was killed in battle and the body lost, they replaced his spirit with the scalp of a slain enemy. Scalps were kept only until a scalp dance was held to celebrate a victory. They were given to their woman folk as if to say that now the fallen warriors' spirit could unite once again with his body. Top this they would dance and rejoice.

One of the most respected acts of bravery was counting coup. This happened when an enemy was touched with a hand, bow or special stick. Another act of bravery was to slip into the camp of the enemy and cut loose a horse tied to a teepee. Another was to lead a successful war party or snatch a bow during hand-to-hand contact, and rescuing a fallen comrade.

Little was said as the tribe made its way rapidly over the plain. Occasionally, as they dashed across a ravine, they suddenly came upon a herd of antelope or a few scattering buffaloes, startling them from their rest and causing them to wonder what the occasion was and who were the strange parties disturbing the peaceful quiet of the night in this manner. On Buffalo Hide and his tribe sped, snuffling the early morning air and pressing forward eagerly as if they knew what was awaiting them.

CHAPTER 19

A Buffalo Mousetrap

As the tribes people traveled toward the west what is now Missouri, the size of the trees diminished as well as the number of different kinds. As you penetrate the plains further, the sight of forests is no longer enjoyed. The only trees to be seen are scattered along the banks of the streams, these became smaller and more rare. Finally, they disappeared altogether and gave place to a few scattering willows and osiers, a willow having long rod like twigs used in basketry. Perhaps this was because of the high winds that prevented in unobstructed force that prevented the growth and existence of, not only trees but also taller grasses. Unlike the Western prairies, that grass attained a height sufficient to conceal a man and a dog pulling a travois. The Plains were covered by a grass, which rarely, and only under favorable circumstances, exceeded three inches in height.

From the grass came repetitive bubbling, flute-like notes varying in length and getting faster at the end.

Shee-oo-e-lee! Shee-ee le-ee!

At a closer look, Buffalo Woman and her sisters saw a meadowlark as they separated the grass. The sound inspired Buffalo Woman to sit down and share with her sisters still another quaint story about the meadowlark passed down from her ancestors. Despite its shy and elusive nature, the meadowlark was well known to the children of the tribe from their storehouse of myths.

It said:

At the beginning of the world all the birds were gray, but through various transformations they came to their present coloring. One day, a little ole man with rather gorgeously colored clothes of yellow, brown, black, and white, was tramping through the fields, when one of the myriads of gray birds circling down flew down and landed on the his hat. The little fairies, laughing and dancing in a nearby field, saw the bird and clapped their hands in glee. At last a wise looking little fairy spoke, and this is what she said: "We have tried so hard to help make this world better and more beautiful that I have just been wondering if I might suggest something to the queen." The queen, a most charming little midget, was present and readily gave her consent, for she was very eager to do all she could to help make everything good and attractive.

"Well," began the fairy who had first spoken, "as I stood here watching that bird on that funny man's hat I just wondered why we couldn't change its gray feathers into those nice colors of the man's coat and other clothes. They are really too bright for him to wear, and they would look beautiful on the bird."

For a minute the queen stopped and looked more closely at the approaching man, with the bird still sitting on his shabby black hat, and then she raised her wand and waved it.

A minute later the plain little gray bird had been changed into a meadowlark with a conspicuous black crescent on his breast.

The bird wore no other colors, except those that had been in the clothing the man wore.

"Meadowlarks prefer living in grassy plains and uplands covered with a thick growth of grass or weeds, near water," added Elk-Woman to her sisters. "See, they are eating grasshoppers, their favorite, and beetles."

As aforementioned, the Plains were once covered with forests is the fact that entire trunks of large trees were found in a state of petrifaction on elevated portions of the country and far removed from the streams of water. It was believed that annual fires were created by the Plains Indians in the fall to burn the dried grass and hasten the growth of the pasturage in early spring.

While dwarfed specimens of almost all varieties of trees are found fringing the banks of some of the streams, the prevailing species are cottonwood and poplar trees. Intermingled with these are clumps of osiers. In almost any other portion of the country the cottonwood would be the least desirable of trees; but to the Indian, and, in many instances that have fallen under observation, the cottonwood has performed a service for which no other tree had been found its equal, and that is a forage for animals during the long winter season when snow prevents even dried grass from being obtainable.

Many a long winter the animals existed upon the young bark of the cottonwood tree. It was not unusual for the Plains People to be invariably located upon that point of a stream promising the greatest supply of cottonwood bark, while the stream in the vicinity of the village was completely shorn of its supply of timber, and the village itself was strewn with the white branches of the cottonwood entirely stripped of their bark.

The herbage, the fleshy, often edible parts of plants used for pasturage and found on the principal portion of the Plains, is usually sparse and stunted in its growth. Along the banks of the streams and in the bottom lands there grows, generally in rich abundance, a species of grass often found in the states east of the Mississippi; but on the uplands is produced what is there known as the "buffalo grass," indigenous and peculiar in its character, differing in form and substance from all other grasses. The blade under favorable circumstances reaches a growth usually of three to five inches. Instead of being straight, or approximately so, it assumes a curled or waving shape, the grass itself becoming densely matted and giving to the foot when walking upon it.

Nearly all the grass eating animals inhabiting the Plains, except the elk and some species of deer, prefer the buffalo grass to that of the lowland. The timber on the bottomland affords good cover to both the elk and the deer. Both are often found in large herds grazing upon the uplands, though the grass is far more luxuriant and plentiful on the lowlands. Our domestic animals invariably choose the buffalo grass, and experience proves beyond question that it is the most nutritious of all varieties of wild grass.

The general directions of all streams, large and small, on the Plains, is from the west to the east, seeking as they do an entrance to what is known as the Mississippi. The habits of the buffalo inclined him to graze and migrate from one stream to another, moving northward and crossing each in succession as he follows the young grass in the spring, and moving southward seeking the milder climate and open grazing in the fall and winter.

Throughout the buffalo country are what are termed "buffalo wallows." The number of these is so great as to excite surprise; a moderate estimate would give from one to three to each acre of ground throughout this vast tract of country. These wallows are about eight feet in diameter and from six to eighteen inches in depth, and are made by the buffalo bulls in the spring when challenging a rival for the favor of the opposite sex.

The ground was broken by the force of their hoof. If the challenge is accepted, as usually is, the combat takes place. The one who came out victorious remained in possession of the battlefield and occupied the "wallow" of fresh upturned earth. Here he found it produced a cooling sensation to his hot and gory sides. Sometimes the victory gives possession of the battlefield and drives a hated antagonist away, is purchased at a dear price. The carcass of the victor is often found in the wallow, where his brief triumph has soon terminated from the effects of his wounds. Also, in the early spring during the shedding season, the buffalo resorted to a "wallow" to aid in removing the old coat.

These "wallows" proved of no little benefit to man, as well as to animals other than the buffalo. After a heavy rain they became filled with water, the soil being so compacted the rain was retained. It was not infrequently the case when making long marches that the streams would be found dry, while water in abundance could be obtained from the "wallows." True, it was not of the best quality, particularly if it had been standing long, and the buffalo had patronized the wallows as "summer resorts." On thePlains a thirsty man or beast, far from any streams of water, did not discuss long before he drank the water.

Buffalo Calf, Buffalo Hide, and the remainder of the tribe continued to follow the river until there before them appeared a two hundred feet high bluff. They continued to march, not taking their eyes off the wonder before them.

"Make camp at base of bluff," instructed Chief Number One.

Buffalo Hide led Buffalo Calf directly to an area below the highest point of the bluff.

"Go gather driftwood logs," instructed Buffalo Hide. "Make pen!"

Everyone joined together to construct a pen as large as their whole camp's circle. Carefully the driftwood was stacked several feet high. Buffalo Calf scrambled over the logs. Protruding from the earth were more white shards of chalky bones.

"One hundred times ten of them!" shouted Buffalo Calf. "Thousands!" he added in disbelief. "This must be buffalo trap!" explained Buffalo Calf.

"Many a great herd has been taken here," added Buffalo Hide.

"Run buffalo herd over cliff. They topple two hundred feet downward," said Chief Number One.

"To their death," added Chief Number Two.

All of them looked all the way up the steep, rockbound cliff disguised by the shrubbery that had erupted voluntarily from the granite. It was so high everyone seemed to topple backward as their eyes traveled upward toward the apex of the bluff.

"It sounds easy," continued Buffalo Calf, "but what if they decide to turn back instead of over the cliff?"

"You'll see very soon," convinced Buffalo Hide. "I am the buffalo caller, and you, Beaver-Tail, will be the scout."

Buffalo Calf's and Buffalo Hide's work was cut out for them if they were to have a successful buffalo hunt.

"We need our sleeping robes," said Buffalo Calf.

"We need some dried meat," said Buffalo Hide.

Together they took a good, long drink of water before they began their climb—heir very…very…very long climb to the top of the bluff.

"It isn't long now, Buffalo Calf," confided in Buffalo Hide. "I will show you how it's done. I promise you."

Starting from almost any point near the central portion of the Plains and moving in any direction, one seems to encounter a series of undulations at a more or less remote distance from each other, but constantly in view.

It looks like the waves in the ocean, thought Nelson Paige.

When he viewed this boundless ocean of beautiful living greenery, he pictured these successive undulations as gigantic waves. They were not wildly chasing each other to and from the shore but were standing silent and immovable. The constant recurrence of these waves was quite puzzling to Nelson Paige. After a weary walk several miles, not more than two, he finds himself at the desired point. There he discovers that directly beyond, in the direction he desires to go, rises a second wave, but slightly higher than the first. From the crest of which he must certainly be able to scan the country as far as the eye can reach. There he pursued his course, and after a ride of five miles, he found himself at the crest or divide. He continued to walk only to discover that another, and apparently higher divide rose in the front of him about the same distance. Hundreds, yes hundreds, of miles may be traveled over, and this same effect would be witnessed every few hours.

CHAPTER 20

The Buffalo Caller

"Come, you will be my scout," howled Buffalo Hide to Buffalo Calf.

Uh hm! Uh hm! Uh hm!

The two climbed and climbed and climbed until the last breath of air was sucked from their lungs.

"Finally reach top of bluff," said Buffalo Hide, half winded.

"Look at the strange rocks," pointed out Buffalo Calf with his pointer finger. Before them was a strange configuration of rocks. The formations were created by hills of rock and sod. Grass and weeds had taken over the rocks to the point of strangulation of one another. It had taken years for the hills and rocks to be covered.

"Position two men behind hills," instructed Buffalo Hide. "Place other men in two long lines. Begin at the edge of the cliff and branch out in fan shape."

The distance between the two hills at the edge of the cliff was about three hundred feet apart. While at the end of the two lines it was over one half a mile, the stationing of men created a funnel effect. The lines themselves, too, were about one half a mile in distance. In each line there were hills disguised with growth approximately thirty feet apart.

The ground work was now laid. Next came the ground rules that Buffalo Hide had carefully thought through.

"Easy, is it not so?" asked Buffalo Calf.

"Yes, if you understand!" replied Buffalo Hide.

"Now what do I do?" asked Buffalo Calf.

"You hide behind the first rock pile of the right line. I'll go to the last rock pile in the right line. You wave your robe, and then I'll wave my robe. This will signal the location of the camp," furthered Buffalo Hide.

Buffalo Calf with much respect for his Uncle Buffalo Hide asked no questions and honored his wishes. Nelson Paige joined him at his side.

Buffalo Calf sprawled over the hill nearest him. Few bushes of sage scrambled here, their gray trunks gnarled and twisted like the trunks of the dwarf trees.

Look! Look! The plains slope gently down from the horizon," noted Nelson Paige.

Still, far across the yellow plain something else focused Nelson Paige's attention.

"See the flashes of white," considered Nelson Paige.

"It's antelope, signaling danger by flirting their long, white hair on their rumps," rationalized Buffalo Calf.

"But how do they signal danger?" inquired Nelson Paige.

"White hair catch sun and warn other antelope," accounted Buffalo Calf, "and then they signal in return."

"Have they seen us?" asked Nelson Paige.

"No, they're on guard for coyote," confirmed Buffalo Calf.

Buffalo Calf was a living testimony to how two coyotes would run an antelope, first one hiding in the brush while the other drove the frightened beast in a circle.

"One coyote run antelope many miles and then return him. The second coyote take up chase while first coyote rest," reckoned Buffalo Calf, "and the animal that goes like the wind is all done at the end."

The day wore onward slowly for Buffalo Calf and Buffalo Hide. Eagles soared in the sky, and crickets sang their monotonous chant. Gophers and mice played among the grasses and sage clumps.

"Where are they?" disputed Buffalo Calf to Buffalo Hide. The wait evoked complex emotions in him by the strange and incomprehensible migration of buffalo. He stood gazing in wide-eyed wonder for the buffalo.

"Let's play hoop game," suggested Buffalo Calf to Nelson Paige.

A large wooden hoop was rolled across the ground, while they competed to knock it over with special throwing sticks. It was not enough to knock the hoop over, though.

"Must hoop land on throwing sticks?" questioned Nelson Paige.

"Yes, must touch only non-wood portion, such as thong tying them together, or rawhide strips around the center," instructed Buffalo Calf.

The hoop game had a religious basis. The hoop was constructed from sweet grass and sage. According to tradition, a band of Sioux was facing starvation. One night, a young man was given the sacred hoop game in a vision. When the hoop was first rolled, it left hoof prints in the dirt. The young dreamer informed them that in four days, four buffalo would walk through the camp. He warned them the buffalo must not be harmed.

Four days later the buffalo appeared. Consequently, the starving band members had great respect for the young man and did not bother the buffalo. Shortly after this a massive herd of buffalo was sighted, and the people were able to eat.

Night descended upon the plains, and all missed their absent friends, the buffaloes.

"Who there?" challenged Buffalo Calf at a twig cracking underfoot.

"Friend!" said a voice in a good-natured manner.

A boy from the camp came bearing a pot of clear drinking water and fresh jerky to put the stomach at peace.

"Sleep now!" offered Buffalo Calf.

CHAPTER 21

The Prairie Eats Up the People

It was several days before the buffalo herds moved into this territory, and all the time Buffalo Calf and Buffalo Hide stood their guard.

"They're moving."

"They're on the run."

The thin, dark line of animals moved slowly toward the bluffs in and out of the hollows.

It looks like beads, thought Buffalo Calf.

It was the line breaking apart and gave the illusion of beads floating down the plains. As the beads moved back and forth, the beads formed a mass as they moved together. Thousands of them were needed to create a mass on the plain. Then a part of the herd broke away to graze at the two lines of hills.

The favorite range of the buffalo was contained in a belt of country occupied by the North and South Plains People. The Southern Plains includes groups that live in the present day Arkansas, Oklahoma, and Texas. The Southern Plains embraced seven hundred fifty thousand square miles of mostly rolling, tireless hills and prairies cut by a number of rivers including the Missouri, Mississippi, and the Colorado. Temperatures fluctuated from minus one hundred degrees Fahrenheit in the winter to one hundred degrees in the summer.

The Northern Plains tribes occupied one point five million square miles to include present day Nebraska, Colorado, Wyoming, Montana, North and South Dakota, and the lower portions of the Canadian provinces Alberta, Saskatchewan, and Manitoba. In the North the terrain is more varied than the south by buttes, ravines and columns.

In migrating, if not grazing or alarmed, the buffalo moved in single file, the column generally being headed by a patriarch of the herd, who is not only familiar with the country, but whose prowess "in the field" entitled him to become the leader of his herd.

He maintained this leadership only so long as his strength and courage allowed him to remain the successful champion in any contest on the range.

The buffalo trails are always objects of interest and inquiry to the sightseer on the Plains. These trails made by the herds in their migrating movements were regular in their construction and course as well as excite curiosity. They varied but little from eight to ten inches in width, and usually from two to four inches in depth; their course ran from north to south and were as unvaried as the needle on a compass.

Buffalo Calf sat attentively, waiting for the signal from Buffalo Hide.

"There it is," said Uncle Buffalo Hide, "the signal!"

Then it came—the wave of the robe. Simultaneously, he felt a cricket biting him savagely on his back. Reaching backward to remove the cricket, it relocated itself out of his reach. Standing, he slowly moved his body through the air to remove it.

He waited until he was well below the edge of the bluff, then fast and furiously he waved his robe until he was sure the people in the camp below had seen his signal.

"Tie up the dogs," called Buffalo Woman to the others.

"Don't forget your robe," added another.

To the observer there was no doubt the camp was in action. The dogs were restricted by being tied to the trees so that they would not interfere with the hunt.

"We begin climbing the bluff," said Buffalo Calf.

Nobody spoke a word but collected their robes, or a large, white deer hide. As they reached the top of the bluff, they separated into two groups. Each group crept along one of the lines of mounds, taking their places behind the hills.

"Hill screen two or more of us," offered Buffalo Woman.

The action was so quick that it seemed to Buffalo Calf as though the prairie had eaten the people alive. Soon there was dead silence—there was no movement to be seen anywhere.

"Looks like no one around," said Buffalo Calf. It looked as though there were no human beings within miles.

The buffalo herd was still three miles away, grazing slowly. Then they saw Buffalo Hide. He was out on the plain, between the two farthest hills. At first Buffalo Hide acted like a real buffalo, for with a buffalo robe over him and its stuffed head wagging from side to side he was mistaken for one. To the herd, at first when they happened upon him, they, too, thought that he was one of them. After awhile, an old cow began to question the odd animal with moccasins as feet. She left the herd slowly and grazed toward it, lifting her head from time to time. Then she walked forward and stopped. Another cow from the herd joined her, then another.

"It's working," contemplated Buffalo Hide. Finally, most of the herd was grazing wonderingly at Buffalo Hide. After some time elapsed they became restless, for something was sensed in the air.

"Was this a buffalo or wasn't it?" would be the words if the buffalo could talk.

At first they moved in around Buffalo Hide, now buffalo incognito on a walk. Their tempo became faster and faster until the first old cow was trotting.

There was still about a quarter of a mile between Buffalo Hide and the cow. The replicated buffalo ducked down into a coulee, came up on another rise, and there pretended to graze.

I must do a dance, thought Buffalo Hide to himself. He ducked this way and that "H…h…h! H…h…h! H…h…h!"

Strange noises came from Buffalo Hide. Meanwhile, all the time he moved slowly and closer to the edge of the cliff.

"I've done it," said Buffalo Hide to himself.

By this time the cow was well inside the outer opening of the funnel of hills. Two calves trotted after, then came more cows. A big bull followed, heavy horns peeping from thick brown man, his flanks slate gray.

Boom! Boom! Boom!

It sounded like thunder. Then came buffalo after buffalo after one another, all intent on what was in front of them.

At this point, Buffalo Hide was running between two lines of the hills.

"Here they come," Buffalo Hide yelled as the buffalo gained on him, but only the first few animals could see Buffalo Hide. The middle and the end of the herd was so caught up in the motion of the stampede that they only noticed the back doors of the buffaloes in front of them. Overhead, still clinging to the wooly backs came the buffalo birds that pick the flies and ticks from the great beasts while they wander everywhere with them.

Wherever water is found on the Plains, particularly if it is standing, innumerable gadflies and mosquitoes generally abound. To such an extent do these pests to the animal kingdom exist, that to our thinly coated animals they are intolerable, while the buffalo with his huge, shaggy coat can browse undisturbed. The most determined of these troublesome insects are the buffalo flies; they move in large numbers and so violent and painful were their assaults that an attack had been known to cause a stampede as the result of an attack from a swarm of these flies.

In most of the areas where these flies are found in troublesome numbers, there are also found flocks of starlings, a species of blackbirds. They did this more to obtain a livelihood than to become the defender of the helpless. They perched themselves upon the backs of the animals. When woe faced the hapless gadfly who ventured near, it became a choice morsel for the starlings, standing guard over the buffalo while he grazed.

When the herd was well inside the outer picket lines, the tribesmen from the farthest hills began bustling out from their hiding places, yelling, shrieking, and waving their robes. The cry was shrill and frantic at times, but they were successful in flushing the herd.

Yee…ee…ee! Yee…ee…!

As the last of the herd passed each hill, more tribes people moved out in quick, jerky movements as if to move up and down. This was followed by frantic waving with their hands. The last of the herd was crazed. They were so panic stricken that they pressed forward faster and faster. The weeds and vegetation in their path was down or lacerated. Eagerly, they moved along, now slipping on a rotten log or a loose stone but making headway. The faster they moved signaled to the tribes people to take action. More and more of them popped out of the ground to wave them onward.

The frantic appearance of the tribes people from out of nowhere followed by everywhere became too much excitement for the buffalo. For those in the middle and at the end it became a mad flight. It was pure madness, and the whole herd was terrorized. Buffalo Hide had long since slid into the tall grass and made his way to Buffalo Calf's hill.

"They're blind," said Buffalo Hide to Buffalo Calf, "blind to the end of their journey."

And now, blind to everything, thinking only of getting away, the whole herd thundered past the rock piles. In a steady stream of dark bodies the buffalo went over the cliff, to fall dead on the rocks two hundred feet below.

"And that is a buffalo drive," said Buffalo Hide to Buffalo Calf who was trembling with excitement. The man was wrapping up his buffalo robe, breathing hard from his long run, and he was perspiring in streams of sweat.

"Now our tribe has meat and robes and everything to make it happy for another year. We have taken over four hundred buffalo, enough to last us through the winter. And now let us go down and help with the skinning," said Buffalo Hide.

The tribe people in gathering the necessary tools to slaughter the buffalo who had not met their demise from the fall occupied the next day. There was one thing they would not have to gather. Finding a bear was the least of their worries; as many as a dozen at a time hung around the place, drawn by the scent of red meat.

"Watch out for female with cubs," warned Buffalo Hide. "Bear everywhere especially in the summer. We set trap for bear."

"Who cares how a bear feel?" came the voice of one of the tribes' people.

"Perhaps they do feel," added Buffalo Woman's sister number one.

"Bah! They no fear," added Buffalo Calf.

"Understand fear and death," added sister number three.

"Nonsense!" amended Buffalo Calf.

A pit was dug in depth until it grew deeper and deeper extending just above Buffalo Calf's shoulders. He climbed out and from some hard saplings cut stakes and sharpened them to fine points. With the points sticking upward, he planted them closely to one another in the pit. Next, with fingers moving like the wind, he wove a web of closely-knit weeds and branches to cover the stakes of the manmade deadfall.

Next, they laid out more branches over the pit that they had dug into the ground. In the center, the branches were covered by deerskins that they wore when they went hunting. Next, they placed a freshly killed jackrabbit under the skins, along with a ball of lard that they soaked with the medicine woman's sleeping potion. It was now just a question of how long it would take for one to appear.

Buffalo Calf and the others were wet with sweat and aching with tiredness. They crouched behind a tree stump that had been charred by lightning. They didn't have to wait long. An abrupt sound startled him. Off to the right Buffalo Calf heard it, and his ears, expert in such matters, could not be mistaken.

Momentarily startled by the sound, he knew that he had new things to learn about fear. He sprang up and moved quickly in the direction from which the sounds came. He leaped upon a rock, trying to balance himself there for a better look. They didn't have to wait long when the padding sound of feet could be heard on the earth. A bear came ambling up. It was a male bear, a shaking mass of fat and dark brown fur waddling from side to side with unexpected agility and grace. His mild curiosity and disposition did in no way deceive the boys as to the bear's capabilities. They were not going to let the bear's attitude cloud their defenses.

Buffalo Calf and the others hoped the breeze would now carry their scent in the direction of the bears. The behemoth made a couple of circles around the area and then smelled the dead jackrabbit. It rose up on its hind legs and stretched out its front paws as it clawed menacingly at the air. There it stood before them; a giant several heads taller than the tallest tribes person. It left out a menacing roar, which froze the blood in their veins. Momentarily, it froze and then it hurled its enormous weight upon the deer hide, smashing through the branches that held it in place. The bear was temporarily dazed at finding itself flat on all fours on the ground in a spread eagle position.

Springing upward without hesitation, again he pawed at the deer skins, and then he discovered the hidden jackrabbit, and the ball of lard saturated with the sleeping potion. In no time he devoured the ball of lard with a large noisy swallow, followed by the jackrabbit. Shredding the deer hide as if in anger, he rose to his full height and searched around in fury when he could not find substantial food. He took a step forward, and began to stagger as if drugged.

Sleep potion work, Buffalo Calf observed.

The bear took another step forward, and with a blink of the eye he tumbled into the pit that Buffalo Calf and his tribe had dug. To their good fortune the bear was dazed by the medicine woman's potion and the impact of the fall. The frustrated roars of the bear gradually seemed to die until they turned into sighs of resignation, and finally he could no longer be heard.

An apprehensive night crawled in like a snake from which blood had been drawn. The silence of the dead world was on their camp. Way into the morning until the sky was veneered with a murky gray, the cry from a startled bird focused Buffalo Hide's attention to the task at hand.

"Let the skinning begin," roared Buffalo Hide.

CHAPTER 22

Cup-caking

Ping! Ping! Ping!

There came a faint sound! Something was being pelted against Nelson's windowpane. This was followed by a laugh and then a giggle in a half-suppressed or nervous manner.

Heah! Heah! Heah!

The successive levels of laughter and giggling were coming from the mulberry tree. A big tree with a thick trunk and outstretched branches had grown outside the window. Enveloped in the branches of the mulberry tree were Nelson's friends, Sydney Best and Judd Levin. They flattened themselves out on a broad limb amongst a screen of leaves almost as thick as a canopy. Nelson went closer to his window and looked out. His room was high up on the second floor, which meant they most likely shinnied up the tree trunk. Their shadows at first were black and noiseless patterns, and then the outline of their bodies came into focus.

They had not seen or heard Nelson so he went back to bed and lay down. He tried to put himself back to sleep, but he only achieved a doze as morning came more heavily upon them. He continued to watch his two friends in the branches of the mulberry tree. Uneasiness could be sensed in their demeanor as the sweet reddish, berrylike fruit was being hurled against Nelson's window between fingering it and devouring it.

Purplish stains appeared around their lips and their tongues, but in no way did the discoloration leave them tongue tied.

Ssss…hhh! Ssss…hhh! Ssss…hhh!

The words exchanged between Sydney Best and Judd Levin lost meaning by the time they reached Nelson Paige's ears; nevertheless, a triumphant grin appeared on their faces. Yes, eyes are a window to the soul. And never was this truer than with Judd Levin. He searched deliberately for what seemed like nothing in particular. And then Judd Levin's eyes glinted into dangerous slits as he produced a shard of mirror from his pocket. The sunlight flickered through the leaves before it landed on the mirror and bounced onto Sydney Best's face.

Aiii—ya! Aiii—ya! Nelson Paige mumbled.

There Sydney Best was trying to "cupcake" with Judd Levin who wasn't making the connection. Sydney Best was no longer the runny-nosed kid with four elbows and enough hair for two heads. Even though her looks had improved over the years, she was now twelve and looked slightly better than she did at eleven. However, coyly romantic wasn't on Judd Levin's agenda to date. Obviously, Judd Levin wasn't aware of Sydney's sweet vague affection directed towards him. Her red headed, side long glances and ideas lost their effectiveness when returned glances in the opposite direction. In no way was she to be coined as being bashful when it came to Judd Levin. She seemed more like fourteen going on fifteen.

The early, crisp morning breeze propelled the fine baby hair on her head that was too wispy and short to be braided. Each morning Sydney's mother used a hard-toothed comb to tame her disobedient hair. It wasn't a bright, blazing red; nor was it brick, Irish setter, lobster, clay, or liver-colored, but rather it was strawberry-blonde in color. She would twist and yank her strawberry-blonde hair that topped her freckled face, and two tightly wound pigtails were formed. At the end of each tail was a plastic barrette trimmed with rhinestones that twinkled like numerous stars in the sky. The rhinestones seemed to dance from the reflection of the sun.

Nelson peered through the windowpane that seemed more like a picture frame with a photo of Sydney "cup caking," Judd. Frustrated in her cup caking, she dejectedly removed a bobby pin from her hair and wedged it between her teeth. She wetted her palm and smoothed the hair above her ear, then pushed the pin in again so that it nicked sharply against her scalp flushing up her scalp to a shade of red.

Then the framed photo was turned off by the shard of mirror in Judd's hand by a simple turn in its direction from the sun. The mirror caught the sunlight and reflected directly into Nelson's line of vision blinding him.

Aiii-ya! Aiii-ya! Aii-ya! his face lengthened as he heaved a sigh of impatience that made air hiss through his nostrils.

The reflection cleaned the remaining sleep from Nelson's eyes. Any dreams he was having had to be left in the web of the dream catcher. There sat Judd and Sydney, in the largest and sturdiest limb of the tree, now beckoning to him. From his bed, Nelson listened as his father got ready for work, then he locked the door behind him.

"One—two—three—click!"

Nelson stood on creaking legs and slowly walked to the window so he could capture more fully what his eyes were trying to comprehend. His facial expressions took on a surprised look.

Judd now had his nose pressed against the windowpane like a fish looking outward from its fishing bowl. His broad, flattened nose and slanted, narrow eyes made him appear different. In any case, they reminded Nelson of bamboo leaves until you got to their color, of course, that changed everything. Depending on the lighting his eyes went from gold to green, back to gold, and in between. His low set ears seemed to drag his facial features downward in a sagging state, which was tapered with a stubby chin. Now think how funny Judd would appear if he didn't have a chin. As far as that goes, how funny any one of us would look. Despite what we see as our shortcomings, we are still the crown of creation.

Judd now began to exert his fist upon the pane. With all his invisible strength, Nelson waited patiently. Inside his room was still dark, and his ceiling was filled with shadows, giving Nelson a concealed advantage to the interlopers on the outside of his window. He could see them clearly; however, the images his room were obscure. If only they knew about the dream catcher that held the secrets into another time, space, and proportion. It was one secret he intended to keep to himself.

Slowly, Nelson Paige moved to the window to slide it open to talk to his friends.

"Hey, Nelson! Hey, Nelson! Do you want to go get an Air-Head X-treme?" asked Sydney Best in anticipation.

The suggestion brought a smile to Nelson Paige's face. It conjured up the taste of sour; on the other hand, to Sydney the sharp, sour taste was unpleasant and most of all disagreeable. Sydney's preference was something sweeter to compliment her cup-caking.

Sydney Best knew Nelson Paige's fetish for Airhead X-tremes, and, oh well, Judd liked anything that was X-treme. Surely, this is what it would take to entice Nelson out of his room; however, they didn't know they were competing against the dream catcher.

Carefully, Nelson opened the screen and crowded onto the heavy limb next to where Judd and Sydney were enveloped by lesser branches. Here, the three of them mapped out their strategy for the second day of school.

CHAPTER 23

Off and Running

Shining down the trunk of the tree, Judd dropped onto his BMX bicycle that rested against the mulberry tree. Nelson Paige and Sydney Best followed. They were off to the local 7-Eleven to purchase what else, but an Airhead X-treme for Nelson. The sweetly sour belts were just the vinegar that was needed. There was no need to say goodbye to Ivy on this second day of school because he was vacationing at the Bed and Biscuit for the next three days since Nelson's father was on a business trip taking his mother with him while Nelson was at school. Ivy would be getting special treatment because of the limited number of dogs accepted into an open backyard wired with classical music.

"Nelson, s-c-a-d-a-d-d-l-e! We'll be late?" yelled Judd back to Nelson and Sydney as they dawdled out of the 7-Eleven.

Molding the world around him to his liking, Judd did a wheelie on his bike while they played catch up. He saw things as black and white; therefore, Judd decided what was black and what was white. At times it was difficult for Nelson to like his friend, Judd, without fearing what he might attempt to do next. There were times that he even hated him and knew what he did was not always right.

Judd Levin became frantic in his attempt to be on time for the second day of school. He knew all his privileges would be removed if he received a detention for being late the second day. And truant was a word that didn't set well with his mother's vocabulary. The closer Judd's wrist watch showed to eight o'clock, the more his extreme tendencies surfaced.

"Wo...ah! Wo...ah!"

Judd was off when he saw a United Parcel truck. He grabbed onto the extended bar on the back for a free ride, looking back at Nelson Paige, he beckoned to him to follow.

"Come on, Nelson! Come on! We're going to be late," yelled out Judd Levin.

It was another attempt to synchronize the world of Judd Levin and Nelson Paige in the same way UPS synchronizes the world of commerce on a daily basis. Nelson Paige sped up and connected to the opposite bar on the backside of the truck. The truck pulled them—yes, right to the front door of the school with five minutes to spare before the bell rang. Unfortunately, Sydney was left pedaling merrily along and arrived, too, at the front door of the school just five minutes later.

The bike stands were overflowing with parked bikes, except for some spaces to the complete rear of the stand. The first bell for school was ringing. Ms. Woodson would be waiting for them at the classroom door. Racing to their classroom door, they found their other classmates standing outside. Nelson pushed his way to the front of the line along with Judd.

"Where's Ms. Woodson? Where's Ms. Woodson?" came Nelson's and Judd's voices in unison. They were put out of their countenance when they discovered Ms. Woodson was late. Sydney Best would not be tardy after all, and their daredevil actions with the United Parcel truck were just plain X-treme.

"Ms. Woodson...she...she flushed her keys down the toilet!" came a meek voice.

The only thought that came to Sydney Best's mind was that Ms. Woodson didn't want to be at school anymore than she did; of course, she knew those very thoughts were true for Judd Levin and Nelson Paige, not so much Nelson as for Judd.

"They fell off her lanyard," added another.

"And she flushed them down," added another in disguised disappointment.

"But it was an accident!" retorted Ms. Woodson unleashing her frustration and at the same time trying to rise above the circumstances befitting a person in a position of authority.

I cannot see that there is anything very funny," she protested. "If you can't do anything better than laugh at me, I can to elsewhere," she added with tearful eyes.

Nelson stood with his mouth agape as he envisioned Ms. Woodson's classroom keys being sucked away by the strength of the flush of the toilet.

Swish! Swish! Swish! And down and away they go.

The power of the flush from the new toilets that had been installed over summer vacation would make it impossible to retrieve them in any way or form. Nelson could only envision them traveling through disposal pipes until they finally came to rest at the local waste disposal plant. Nelson's thoughts about the swirling motion of the water and the force of the water from the flush were soon interrupted by the voice of the school principal looking somewhat agitated but in control.

"Okay! Okay! Okay, boys and girls!" came a voice in utmost coolness.

It was the principal with Ms. Woodson following tightly at his rear.

"FIDO! *FIDO!*" Ms. Woodson!" the principal, Mr. Ballard, said to her to help her gain control of herself and lighten the intensity of the moment.

Mr. Ballard always used the acronym to calm his rookie teachers in situations like this one. It simply meant *forget it drive on*. It was simple to Mr. Ballard: every day somebody, something pulls us off course.

"Remember FIDO: *Forget it drive on*," he reiterated to Ms. Woodson the action to be taken. "*Fido! Fido!*"

With those words of inspiration nothing would let the second day of school from not happening for Ms. Woodson. With his master key in hand, Mr. Ballard inserted the key into the lock.

Cl...ick! Cl...ick!

The key rotated the lock cylinder, and the door pulled open on its hinges to reveal everything under lock, stock, and barrel.

Yeah! Yeah!

The students flocked through the door with Ms. Woodson at the end like a caboose. In seconds the desks were filled, and everyone was ready for her to impart words of wisdom and knowledge upon which to build their lives and world visions.

It was evident that Ms. Woodson had spent several hours the previous day after school preparing for this day. In her most perfect script, Ms. Woodson had scrolled upon the whiteboard word for word with her black Expo felt-tipped pen sayings that transported subliminal messages to the reader, messages for the students to contemplate. Nelson had never seen the whiteboards so full of information during the previous year. Perhaps this was an indication that he was one year older and bigger, and better things were expected of him. After all it was all about ***expectations***!

Boys of good habit are most likely to secure positions of trust.

The best way to turn off the edge of a joke is to join the laugh yourself.

Stay well is good!
Do well is better!

Think before you ink.

"People who are wrapped up in themselves make small packages."

It's not how well you look, but how you behave.

"We grow too old soon and too late smart."

Notice all clock watchers, time passes but will you?

Nothing is work unless you would Rather be doing something else.

Have no fear of tomorrow, God is already there.

Never speak of a man's virtues before his face and his faults behind his back.

A friend is like a rare copy of which there is one copy.

Virtue is the only true nobility.

Smiles beget friends and Friends are better than fortune.

People who throw dirt lose ground.

To be rather than to see!

Honesty is the best policy.
Happiness, of course, lies within,
But happiness is not what you have or have not,
Happiness is the ability to appreciate what is around you.
If anyone looks far enough he will have much around him about which to be happy.

What you are to be you are now becoming.

Times were good for Mahogany Woodson. Times were bad for Mahogany Woodson. Times were foolish for Mahogany Woodson. The incredulity of what had transpired the second day of school before beginning her class made her speechless. Before this event in her day she had everything before her short of nothing. Now she felt despair along with hope that the principal would be forgiving.

"Good morning, boys and girls," articulated Ms. Woodson in her most perfect phonetic pronunciation carefully yielding perfect morphemes to deliver her message. Nelson watched her lips. They moved in perfect beat, sound, accent, and motion. The relative length and accent of the words were music to the ears of her students.

"I'm going to be your teacher this year. With a name like Woodson you probably think I should be a carpenter and teach woodshop. And with a first name like Mahogany that makes me a carpenter who has a strong liking for mahogany, a wood the color of my hair, reddish brown. However, I am your teacher for this school term. The first thing on the agenda for today is to collect your class schedules."

For the second day of school minimal day was in effect. This shortened schedule was putting her under the gun to keep the ball rolling as the saying goes. Class schedules were reviewed until Ms. Woodson came to Judd.

"Where's your class schedule, Judd?" pressed Ms. Woodson in a hurried tone of voice.

"Judd forgot it!" came a sweet but vague voice in front of him.

"Ouch! Don't do that!" Judd had yanked Sydney Best's strawberry-blonde pigtail in an attempt to silence her.

"Oh, Mr. Forgetful," replied Ms. Woodson. "You need to report to Mr. Coles for lunch detention."

"But it's a shortened day!" wailed Judd Levin.

"Sorry!" retorted Ms. Woodson with her reddish-brown hair perfectly styled.

As Ms. Woodson sized him up and down from head to toe, in her appraisal he would have to be remade almost entirely, but, fortunately, she had good raw material with which to work. By any means, he wasn't going to be a turtle dove in her hand she considered further, while the same time smiling at him amiably.

Nelson sat in his desk looking first at Ms. Woodson's words written on the whiteboard upon which she molded her teaching and then back at Judd. Judd was a friend and a *rare copy*, and there was only one of him—he had no doubt. There weren't too many people like him. X-treme and singular he was all wrapped up in the same package.

"Mr. Coles, I'm not afraid of that dumb harelip!" whispered Judd to Nelson, exposing his insensitive nature as he crossed his arms over his chest scornfully.

The only thought that could go through Nelson's mind was that his friend was a dithering imbecile; but then again emotion did have its place. Hopefully, Judd would consider his position as a student and keep his remarks to himself.

"He'll have you screaming like a baby," returned Nelson to his friend laughingly.

CHAPTER 24

The Treasure Chest

Next on the agenda for Ms. Woodson's class was the Treasure Chest situated on a shelf at the side of the room.

"I wonder what's in the chest?" queried Sydney, making a ninety degree turn in her seat to make sure he was paying attention to her question.

There it sat with a lock to be opened by the three students who drew the lucky key from the basket that held a total of 500 keys.

"Ms. Woodson…Ms Woodson! What's in the chest?" came Sydney Best's inquiry as she raised herself off her seat and waved her hand to get Ms. Woodson's attention.

"There are small envelopes, and in each envelope there is a treasure," returned Ms. Woodson.

Sydney Best's eyes became as big as saucers. Just the sight of the chest conjured images of pirates and the Dead Man's Chest. Sydney dreamt of being dressed with diamonds, rubies, emeralds, and even sapphires. Judd, on the other hand, imagined himself being confronted by one-eyed Jack, and Nelson was the captain of the pirate ship. At any rate, it took them on a journey to far away places filled with mystery and adventure.

Ms. Woodson began to go into detail about how the treasure hunt would take place in the classroom. Walking around the room, she placed a discipline dollar into the hands of each student, and in their other hand she placed what appeared to be a scroll that was held together by a ribbon.

"It's a Dead Sea Scroll," whispered Sydney to Judd, who only listened attentively.

"Now, students, I would like you to open your scrolls and follow along," instructed Ms. Woodson as she read out to them for everyone to hear.

the 2nd day of September in the year 2007

Ahoy Matey,

Starting September 3rd we will be begin our discipline bucks program!

You will be able to win by following classroom discipline policies to create a better learning environment for yourself and your peers.

There are 500 keys in the basket. Some of the keys work, and some of the keys don't work. Each key cost $40.00 of earned discipline bucks. You can win up to forty points or $40.00 worth of discipline bucks a week. Each day is worth eight points.

If your key opens the treasure chest, then you will be able to pick an envelope.. Each envelope contains a number, and the number corresponds with the prize you find printed on the flags.

"Follow the flags, and you will see a special treasure waiting for thee."

Your captain,
Ms. Woodson

"If you turn over your discipline buck now, you will see what rules to be followed if you are to earn a key to open the chest."

Carefully, each student turned over his discipline buck to see what made up a classroom violation.

```
                    CLASSROOM VIOLATIONS


Student's Name:_____

Discipline Report by: Ms. Woodson

Infraction Issues:

_____Cheating_____Lying_____Disrespect_____Defiance

_____Swearing_____Eating in Class_____ 3 tardies _____no electronics

Remarks:_____

_____Verbal Warning            Date Given:

_____Written Warning           Date Given:

_____Telephone home:           Date Given:


Date:_____

Incident:_____

Student Signature:
```

"If you get no checks, do we get eight points?" asked Sydney Best waving her hand as she perched herself on the end of her chair. Ms. Woodson nodded her head in affirmation to her question.

"Eight points a day times five days a week equals forty points or $40.00," assured Ms. Woodson with a smile. "Them you have earned a key to the treasure chest. If the key opens the chest, you choose an envelope. The number inside the envelope matches a number on a flag to a prize."

The entire class sat quietly like ice sculptures that you could see through to the visions dancing in their heads about the contents of the treasure chest. A quick glance at the hands on the clock pressed Ms. Woodson to move onward.

"Notice, all clock watchers, time passes but will you?" verbalized Nelson to himself as he read from Ms. Woodson's truths. Time was passing for Ms. Woodson.

Quickly she distributed books to each student, carefully assigning a book number to each student.

"Sydney, your book number is x216287."

"Judd, you are assigned book number x321908.

"Nelson, number X345987 is the barcode on your book." She continued assigning numbers until all thirty students received a number aligned with a book.

"Ms. Woodson…Ms.Woodson, if we lose the book do we have to pay for it?" came a voice from the corner of the room.

"Yeah!" What do you think stupid," came another voice.

"What if we write in it?" asked still another voice.

"Or tear a page?" came another voice.

"Look at this one. It has bubble gum inside the cover."

"I'm going to pass out a book claim and on the book claim check the condition of the book: good, new, or used.

_____GOOD_____NEW_____USED

"Each and every one of you needs to sign your book receipt," finalized Ms. Woodson in a melodious tone of voice. "If there are any damages to the book, please note them on the book claim.

With this activity completed for the second day of school, the bell sounded. Judd reported for detention to Mr. Coles; consequently, Sydney Best would not be cup-caking with Judd Levin today in the mulberry tree. And Nelson high tailed it out of there to take over where he'd left off with his dream catcher.

CHAPTER 25

Wings of the Wind

Nelson Paige seemed to fly home after the second day of school. He knew he had free and full reign of the house since his mom had accompanied his dad on a business trip.

Taking two steps at a time to expedite his climb to his upstairs bedroom, he arrived breathless but ready to see the dream catcher once again at work. He couldn't wait to meet up with Buffalo Calf. Little did he know that he was in for more distant travel into time, space, and proportion.

"Buffalo Calf go to Happy Hunting Ground!"

To be exact, it was one hundred years later, and numerous changes had taken place on the Plains. Buffalo Calf had grown up to be a brave warrior and hunter, just like his Uncle Buffalo Hide. He had children, grandchildren, and great grandchildren. The tribe had become so large that they had to divide into two tribes. One tribe stayed, but the other went West toward the mountains.

"I see white man!" said Nelson Paige further perplexed, "No, wait, wait; they are Spaniards."

The Spaniards had come from the far, far south, in Mexico.

"Look they're riding big dogs! There are hundreds of them."

They brought horses from Europe, and the horses had colts that grew up until there were great herds of horses. Some of the horses broke away from their owners and fled into the canyons. Here they gave birth. Some one hundred years after the buffalo hunt, herds of wild horses wandered in the Rocky Mountains and the Great Plains. The buffalo, elk, and antelope had to now share their space with the wild horses. Plains People soon learned to ride the big dogs by watching the Spaniards. The Plains People could teach the People of the North.

Buffalo Calf's great grandchildren only heard stories about great grandfather Buffalo Calf who went on Buffalo hunts with his dogs. Instead of walking weary miles, Buffalo Calf's grandchildren and great grandchildren could sit on a horse and go here, there, and everywhere. Buffalo Calf's offspring could ride further in one day than they could walk in five and could carry heavier material than the dogs could even pull.

"What a new idea this is!" was the talk amongst the villagers. It spread like wildfire. Everyone wanted to join in the new idea. To make this a reality, horses were stolen, and others were traded. Soon all the villages had horses, and their habits changed completely.

"What need now?" came the exchanges between Buffalo Calf's offspring.

"No need to huddle in one place in dark, gloomy earth lodges."

"We have wings of the wind to carry us anywhere."

So they left their lodges to be washed away by the rain or be torn down by the winds. The horse to the Sioux was a dream machine. Now buffalo hunts could be controlled. Mounted on the horse they could now control the quality and quantity of buffalo killed. Guiding his horse with his knees, a Plains hunter approached a herd of buffalo easing his mount along a preferred cow or young bull and discharged an arrow.

The Plains People could now find distinction through battle through a full scale offensive. Traveling at speeds of forty miles plus an hour they were skilled enough to notch their bowstrings with arrows.

It was the foundation for war in their culture. Horses became mystery dogs, medicine dogs, sacred dogs and even big dogs.

A family with a hundred or more horses was believed to be wealthier than one with only a few. It is believed that the arrival of the horse let to the destruction of the buffalo. Before the European arrival in America and the horse, it was estimated there were sixty million plus buffalo. By the 1900s the number was down to the five hundreds.

CHAPTER 26

Tinkling Bell

Buffalo Calf's great grandchildren were part of the tribe that formed in the North. It was from one of these families that an unusually beautiful girl was born. She was about to walk in her ancestor Buffalo Calf's footsteps.

"We make teepee," Tinkling Bell said to her mother. Just as Buffalo Calf made a teepee of seven buffalo hides, she would make a teepee of twenty buffalo hides.

"Teepee largest of the tribe," said Tinkling Bell as she stood back marveling and rejoicing at her accomplishment with her mother. It was not like her ancestors tiny shelter that wobbled on its bending poles but rather majestic in proportion.

"Mustang drag on travois," instructed Tinkling Bell.

A wiry, strong mustang dragged the twenty buffalo skin construction into position. It was exactly the same shape as Buffalo Calf's, but the poles were longer and the round frame for carrying it was bigger.

"Teepee stand up stout and strong on poles," pointed out Tinkling Bell.

"It's like a bowstring!" a comparable point made by her mother.

"Look, no sags or ripples!" applauded Tinkling Bell.

The big tent sat squarely into position just as Tinkling Bell and her mother had planned. Means of ground conveyance were different too than they were in Buffalo Calf's day.

"Look! Look!" Tinkling Bell called in her loudest whoop as a wagon overflowing with beaver furs passed in front of them.

The ground vehicle was originally a circular frame or disk, constructed to revolve a central axis. It was a wheel but not the first one known to civilization. The earliest known wheels, constructed in ancient Mesopotamia, date from about 3500 to 3000 BC. Wheeled vehicles are believed to have appeared after the invention of the potter's wheel, and the wheeled cart soon replaced the sledge as a means of transportation. In its simplest form, the wheel was a solid, wooden disk mounted on a round axle to which it was secured by wooden pins. Eventually sections were carved out of the disk to reduce the weight, and radial spokes were devised about 2000 BC. The invention of the wheel was a major turning point in the advance of human civilization. The wheel led to more efficient use of animal power for agriculture and other work; it became an invaluable mechanical means for controlling the flow and direction of power or force. The application of the wheel in modern life and technology are virtually infinite.

So too the travois had been replaced by the more efficient use of the wagon. Tinkling Bell and her people had never seen a wagon on wheels. But some of the bravest men had journeyed far to the south on their horses, loaded with beaver furs, and had traded with these people face to face. They negotiated items of like value in their transactions.

"For a pile of skins as high as my knees, buy an iron knife!"

"For pile as tall as our belts, give a tomahawk with a steel head!"

"For other piles, trade glass beads."

The glass beads were as small as the eyes of mice, with holes clear through them so they could be sewn in designs like porcupine quillwork, only much faster.

Just think! For only as many thick beaver skins as a very strong horse could carry, one could buy a whole basket of beads.

Tinkling Bell stood amazed as the multi-colored beads poured through the traders fingers in all colors—bright red, yellow, blue, white, and black. Tinkling Bell's father, Painted Face was one of these gifted traders. He had a gift of bargaining, and a good one at that.

"No one get the better of me!" howled Painted Face to his daughter Tinkling Bell. "Have presents for everyone!" rhapsodized Painted Face to Tinkling Bell and his other family members and friends.

For fifty horses and pelts for the last five years of hard trapping, he had come home loaded with the purchases he had made for all of them.

"For Tinkling Bell and the other women folk here are all the beads needed for their white buckskin dresses," Painted Face noted. "For my boys have red cloth—think of it—for their breech cloth," he needled. "Not only this, bargain for brass bells," Many-Painted-Ponies lashed out to all those gathered around.

"Ring-a-ling! Ring-a-ling!" rang the twenty brass bells as Tinkling Bell held them upward in a swinging motion.

The hollow metal object, shaped like an upside down cup, made a ringing sound when it was hit by a piece of metal that hangs down inside it. It was the brass bells that gave Tinkling Bell her name.

"I'll tie them to my dress!" expounded Tinkling Bell as she tied them tightly to her best dress, below the belt, with strong thongs made from sinew. "I'll ride with the wind!" she giggled.

And when she climbed into her bright saddle on her spotted pony and rode away, the whole tribe heard her.

Tinkle… Tinkle… Tinkle!

The bells tinkled as if to sing a song:

> ***Tinkling bells sing your song,***
>
> ***Tinkling bells sing loud and clear.***
>
> ***Your sweet chime let us hear.***
>
> ***Tinkling bells keep her free from fear.***

The tinkling of the twenty brass bells seemed to make her spotted pony go faster and faster and faster; Tinkling Bell giggled and giggled and giggled, adding to the merriment of the moment.

"This not the high feather of Painted Face's gift giving," offered Tinkling Bell.

Indeed, this was not the crowning glory of his gift giving. The crowing glory was something Painted Faces gave himself.

"You hold horn," he instructed a brave, as he took black powder from a funny new kind of horn.

"I put black powder in barrel and push with a stick," he further instructed.

After ramming down some round pieces of heavy metal and pulling a little stick at the bottom of the wood, he made thunder and lightning.

Boom! Bang! Bang! Boom!

The sound echoed through the air, leaving a trail of smoke that followed its path.

Thump!

A buffalo fell dead at a greater distance than it would have been possible to shoot him with an arrow!

"I try out on my way back from the journey," explained Painted Face.

"No more bows and arrows for Painted Face.

"Come, my friends, make big circle on the outskirts of teepees," instructed Painted Face. It was here that he began his speech about the new magic. "Here this bow and arrow for you," he said, as he handed it to a brave that stood near in great anticipation of what was to follow.

"Now I have a new weapon!" he informed his friends who stood impressed but in silence at what would be Painted Face choice of weapon for the tribe.

"Again pour magic powder into tube," he said as he opened the magic horn and poured the powder into the metal tube.

He poured carefully, measuring the stream of powder as it flowed. He kept pouring until he was sure there was enough.

"Now I pull little stick," he informed his onlookers who had moved even closer to him s o as not to miss any step in the preparation of the weapon to fire.

Bang! Bang! Bang!

Such a thunder!

Crash! Crash! Crash!

Such a lightening split the air!

"I smell powder!" nasalized Tinkling Bell, as the explosive powder entered into the atmosphere. A great cloud of bad smelling smoke rolled up.

"Where's Painted Face?" asked Tinkling Bell.

When his friends now saw him, he was sitting down in the grass, looking at the magic stick.

"Something go wrong," mumbled Painted Face as he sat looking at the bent metal tube that now was completely full of cracks.

"Magic stick never kill buffalo again," gulped Painted Face as he stared at the magic stick; nevertheless, he had a drawing together to the old weapon. Whenever there was a dance in the village, Painted Face could be seen dancing with the old stick hooked over his shoulder despite the unfortunate coincidence.

"He has one of those White-Man-Magic Sticks," whispered the tribes people amongst each other. This made him stand apart by reason of superior importance. The magic stick was his chief claim to importance. This made him a greater chief than ever.

They were all afraid and stunned and thought the magic stick was powerful, thought Painted Face with quiet conviction.

When he had the magic stick in his possession, he felt secure and recovered a bantering tone that sent the tribes people into madness.

Though, as yet, they hadn't discovered how the magic stick functioned. This was the first gun these people had ever heard. They were not to hear another for many years. They lived on the Plains, happy without guns. The magic stick would never be as great as the horse.

For quite a while Native hunters shunned the use of guns because the noise panicked the herds. Warriors, however, quickly adopted firearms and developed creative techniques for using them on a galloping horse. In action the Plains warrior held the fire until his enemy was in a close range, but he learned to reload rapidly by carrying the balls in his mouth and spitting them down the gun barrel.

Unfortunately, firearms changed Plains warfare into a much bloodier and lethal affair, for the powerful new weapons made possible the killing and maiming of far greater numbers of people as well as the buffalo population. Between 1860 and 1870 most of the major battles of Northern and Southern Plains People were fought. The Cheyenne formed an alliance with the Sioux and the Arapaho and fought an on going war with the U.S. military. Probably the most notable known was the Battle of the Little Bighorn, in which the Sioux and Cheyenne warriors met the forces of General George Custer. Sitting Bull and Crazy Horse led the counter attack that resulted in the deaths of Custer and all his men.

Some of the tribes, like the Sioux and Blackfeet, had special warriors called sash bearers. The sashes trailed over one shoulder to the ground. During the battle a sash wearer staked himself to the earth. This was a signal to the other warriors that he would die rather than retreat. Once the warrior committed himself there was no turning back unless the whole group decided to withdraw. Then the stake could be removed, and the wearer with the sash freed.

After the wars the Plains tribal leaders who were considered always bad, were given white man's haircuts and clothing, and the missionaries converted them to Christianity changing their lives forever in a new direction.

CHAPTER 27

The Wings of Time

"We follow buffalo on wings of the wind," Painted Face prompted to his friends whose skin had burnt to a wood tone. No matter where the buffalo went now, they could follow him on the wings of the wind, from the open plains to the Rocky Mountains.

"This summer we wander over the eastern part of the Great Plains," announced Tinkling Bell to the members of her tribe. "Next, we move west again."

The string of horses seemed endless…black ponies…white ponies…bay ponies…brown ponies…painted ponies…spotted ones in two or more colors trotted along over the yellow prairie.

"Long ago, when our ancestors march, women and children make central column. With them were horses, using the same sort of travois that the dogs had used, but, of course, much larger. Herd boys in the rear took care of the many extra horses. In front rode the chiefs, as before. There was the same formation of warriors at the sides and rear as a guard, and far out ahead, miles in advance, rode the scouts," contributed Painted Face.

The great train was now passing a low bluff. On this bluff Tinkling Bell could see against the sky, low, rambling mounds standing out. Tinkling Bell watched tentatively as the formation of the tribe changed.

"At my signal you leave women and ride out through the warriors and meet me trotting toward the mounds," he instructed Tinkling Bell as he pointed in the direction of the massive dirt hills.

"Here, my daughter, is an abandoned village such as our people used in the days before we had horses," Painted Face said to his daughter, Tinkling Bell. As he talked, the passion of his conversation caused him to draw close in beside her until their stirrups touched. In Tinkling Bell's mind no one was superior by their ancestry or birth, only for their wisdom and courage like her father Painted Face.

"But isn't your tribe still alive?" asked Tinkling Bell.

"Oh, yes," replied Painted Face, "and the people still live in their earth lodges further east on the Great River known today as the Missouri River"

"Lodges have changed since I was a boy," added Painted Face to Tinkling Bell.

With the coming of the horses those very same lodges had changed their dimensions, and they became larger.

"Now, in one lodge there is room, not only for a family and relatives, but also, sometimes, for as many as twenty of the best ponies. Unlike this ancient village we're coming to was built in the days when its inhabitants had only dogs. I want you to look over the ruins and see how times have changed since then," instructed Painted Face.

"We stop here," announced Painted Face to his daughter.

They reigned in their lodges on a knoll and looked down.

"See the gray poles poking upward through the sod, all that was left of the stockade," expounded Tinkling Bell's father.

She could see the roofs of the lodges had fallen in, but some of the sturdy center poles still stood upright.

"Look over there, earth from roofs had made low hills and are covered with grass," said her father.

"Oh look, Father! You can see the trails among the mounds left by the buffalo."

Tinkling Bell and Painted Face began to ride their ponies for several yards until they began to share thoughts with each other again.

"How lonely it looks," said Tinkling Bell.

"It's hard to believe that this used to be a village inhabited by people who walked far out on the plains, slaughtering as many buffalo as possible at one time, dragging the dried meat home with the dogs," added Painted Face.

"Life must have been very hard in those days," returned Tinkling Bell.

"Yes, it was a hard life," replied Painted Face, "but it was a good life, too."

"How so," asked Tinkling Bell quizzically.

"A man had to be hard like my iron knife then," said Painted Face, "and he had to be a good runner."

Painted Face had heard tales about Buffalo Calf, when he grew to manhood; he ran eighty miles between sunrise and sunset, on a bet.

"How far was that?" asked Tinkling Bell.

"Course out to a hunting camp and back, forty miles each way. When he came sprinting through the stockade gates, the people cheered from the lodge roofs. Straight to the dancing circle he ran, and, to show off, leaped over a pile of buffalo skulls. He landed right in a puddle of mud, but he did not mind the laugher this caused because he knew that no one else in the tribe could have done what he had done. He won twelve big dogs on that bet."

"Wow!" responded Tinkling Bell as she tentatively listened to her father's recollection of his ancestor Buffalo Calf.

"In these days," he went on, "what do our warriors do now?

Ride! Ride! Ride!

Tinkling Bell sat quietly waiting for Painted Face to impart some truths to her upon which to guide her life.

"It's hard to make one of our young men walk twenty feet if there is a horse handy."

"But horse makes life different," Tinkling Bell imparted to her father.

"Horse makes soft meat of our men," contradicted her father.

Of course, they could fight and ride for a week at a time, changing their horses at the camps and eating in the saddle.

"What is that to compare to Buffalo Calf," questioned Painted Face.

"*Perhaps, after all, the good old days were the best!*" thought Tinkling Bell briefly.

"Well, Father," replied Tinkling Bell with a smile at the corner of her mouth, "if you think walking is such healthful exercise, look out there."

Painted Face turned around on his horse to see a train of his people just a line in the distance.

"Now, I'll lead your horse, and you can trot back on foot. You might catch up by morning," noted Tinkling Bell as her father's expression turned to one of deepening concern.

"And that's another thing. The younger generation is getting more disrespectful every day," he said, pretending to be angry.

"Anyway," said Tinkling Bell, "I'm glad I'm alive now. I wouldn't like to live in a dark, dingy old earth lodge, having known the fresh air of our teepee, or to stay in one place by a corn patch all my life."

"Corn patch give food to live!" renounced Painted Face.

"I would die if we couldn't … ride and ride and ride seeing our new country, new mountains, and new lakes! Come on, I'll beat you back to the others!" encouraged Tinkling Bell on the arid prairie that looked particularly welcoming. And with a slap of quirts, the ponies spurted forward over the plain.

Two weeks later the tribe reached the foothill country. Already in the West, the great ranges of the Rocky Mountains lay blue against the sky. One morning, Painted Face gathered the other chiefs about him in his teepee.

"Good buffalo country here," he said, as the chiefs situated themselves in a circle contemplating what Painted Faces was up to?

"All around the open plains before us are ravines and arroyos. We could surround a herd out there without being seen by the buffalo," pointed out Painted Face to the chiefs.

"We need fresh meat!" interjected another chief.

"We can store supplies of dried meat here for use when we come back this way next winter or spring," suggested still another chief. Their argument was too great for incident. The prospect of death was a strong motivation for the chiefs.

"Besides, it's time the women make pemmican," came words of wisdom from the last chief with sallow eyes, a sickly pale yellow.

"He speaks with a wise tongue," said Sleeps-On-The Pony, taking his turn at the passed around pipe.

There were different types of pipes by the Native nations. Some pipes were made of wood others a special kind of stone. Some pipes were plain with no decorations, like the one smoked by Painted Face and the chiefs. Some were painted and trimmed with fur, quills, beads, and eagle feathers and decorated with carvings. Tobacco and red willow bark were used to fill the pipe.

"Let the hunt begin!" decided the chiefs as Painted Face took his last puff.

CHAPTER 28

The Buffalo Robe

Camp was pitched in a river valley out of sight of the open country. The teepees were white specks in the thickets of willows and cottonwoods. The horses were hidden down in low grass lands.

"See nothing! Where are the buffalo?" questioned a brave to one of the chiefs.

With nothing in sight for days, the buffalo had fled before the moving Natives, began drifting back into the country.

"Again time for hunt," said Painted Face one night. Leading the party, he began the hunt.

"Ride quietly so not disturb grazing buffalo," he told the members of his hunting party.

They rode along the bottoms of the coulees, and by morning they had surrounded the grazing buffalo.

"Look! Look! Over there!" invoked Painted Face to the members of the hunting party as he pointed at the smoke signal from a watcher on a high butte. Several of the members dismounted their ponies and crawled combat style to get a closer look to see the buffalo.

"Let's close in," yelled out Painted Face to the hunting party.

"Here, take buffalo robe," said one hunting party member.

"Here's one for you," said another, as he passed the buffalo robe on.

"Here's another one," said still another member of the hunting party.

This went on for a period of time until all the buffalo robes were distributed to everyone.

"Draw the corners together," instructed one member.

"Sit on them so that the skin cannot slip off," instructed another member to the others.

As they left their horses grazed toward the herd, they sprawled over the necks of the ponies.

"Now look like humped buffalo," Painted Face made known to everyone in a buffalo robe.

The buffalo robes seemed to be working. The animals took no alarm to the members of the hunting party as they took their positions for the capture.

An hour passed…

then another…

then another…

still another!

At length, the buffalo sensed something was wrong. The watcher on the butte became pensive. Stampeding at any moment was a likely scenario because the buffalo, too, were becoming restless.

Attack! Attack! Attack!

The signal from the butte was given and the members of the hunting party trotted forward in pursuit of the buffalo.

Stampede! Stampede! Stampede!

The buffalo did not know which direction to turn. In every direction there were riders. The outer animals headed for the middle and all milled about in confusion.

"Throw back your robes!" roared Painted Face, as he tore the buffalo robe from his body and headed in the direction of the buffalo.

"Charge down the flanks of the herd!" came the second directive from their chief.

Arrows came from all directions as they charged down the flanks of the herd, pouring arrows into the mass of brown bodies as fast as they could notch them.

"They're breaking," hollered Painted Face to the top of his voice.

The buffalo broke and ran in all directions; nevertheless, the horses were fresh. Painted Face and the members of the hunting party steered them by the pressure of their knees only, freeing up their hands to use their weapons.

"Every man for himself!" thundered Painted Face to the rest of the hunters. Each rider followed a certain group.

Tinkling Bell sat on a hill and watched with wonderment. First she saw a herd like a brown puddle of mud on the yellow plain. When the rider charged, it was though some giant had thrown a great stone that made the puddle splash out at the edges in all directions. She saw a horse close in beside a buffalo. She saw the bow drawn, saw it snap taut again. The buffalo plunged forward and went down, staining patches of the earth crimson. Then the horse spurted forward again to range alongside another buffalo.

"They are dropping by the dozens," she murmured to herself at the sight.

When the arrows were all gone, men used their lances. The tide of brown surged across a flat place, and when it had gone, the ground was dotted with dark mounds. From the hill where Tinkling Bell watched, these mounds looked like strings of beads, all pointing outward from the place where the herd had first stood.

CHAPTER 29

Pemmican

"They're back!" came the voice of the village crier.

"They're back!" cheered the women and children as they came galloping into camp.

"Let the skinning begin," bellowed Painted Face.

"Hoist up the elk and deer," directed a member of the hunting party to the camp members.

"But not the cow buffalo, weigh too much!" Painted Face said, looking incredulous.

Everyone shook their heads in dismay and awe at their triumphant trophy. The cow buffalo weighed about one thousand pounds, and the bulls sometimes a ton, so it was too difficult to hoist them upward.

"Slit buffalo hide along the backbone."

"First lay buffalo on its side."

"Work the skin off the upper side and under the belly."

"Now remove the meat from the side."

"Now turn the buffalo over!"

The remaining hide and meat were taken off. The members of the party worked together in harmony, each contributing to a part of the skinning. All that week the meat was dried in strips in the sun or cured over smoking fires. When it was thoroughly dried, it was hard and weighed less than half as much as when it was fresh.

"Crush large leg bones with stone hammers!"

"Marrow and bone grease boiled in pots and skimmed off."

"We store in cleaned bladders and intestines."

"Some used to make pemmican," interjected Tinkling Bell. "Pound the dried meat with stone hammers until it is fine shreds," instructed Tinkling Bell to the other women, as she joined into the pounding while others gathered more berries to add to the already stored berries. "Mix meat with berries and store for this purpose. Now mix with some of the bone grease! Next put the paste up in the bladder and intestine casings," instructed Tinkling Bell. "Keep for three or four years. Good winter food."

The pemmican went a long way in the diet of the plains people. One spoonful made a meal, rich and well-balanced. It would last an entire winter season.

CHAPTER 30

Parfleches

Enough meat to last for a journey was stored in "parfleches." These were rawhide covered bundles, folded like a flat suitcase, which were to be carried with the tribe on its wanderings. The remainder was to be left behind.

"Mark out certain spots on bluffs," directed Painted Face as he superintended this job.

Men marked out certain spots on bluffs in preparation to make a hole.

"Now cut each spot, a circle of sod two feet across," further instructed Painted Face.

They lifted the sod out carefully and laid it aside.

"Now dig straight down!"

Following Painted Face's directions, they dug the hole straight down, as though making a hole for a huge post. Two feet down they began scooping outward all around until they had a den like a great pot large enough to hold two men.

"Dig with buffalo shoulder blades!" insisted Painted Face to the diggers.

The dirt was handed up in pots and baskets through the two feet manhole.

"When den large enough, we line with willow brush, dry grass, and finally dry hides," he affirmed to the diggers.

"Lay jerked meat inside and cover with grass, hides, and earth," added Painted Face.

The hole was filled with earth, well packed down, and the sod cover placed back exactly in place. All the earth dug from the den had been kept in hides, and what was left over was thrown into the river.

"Now," said Painted Face to his daughter, "the coyotes and wolves will gnaw the bones down on the plain, but they will not find these storehouses. Neither will our enemies. The meat will keep perfectly for a year or two, and we can always return to this spot if we need food in our wanderings.

Painted Face is a wise father, thought Tinkling Bell.

"We travel tomorrow," he informed the rest of the hunting party.

The week after the storing of the dried buffalo meat, the tribe reached the Rocky Mountains.

"Here we camp through the fall, hunting and trapping for furs along the lakes and stream," instructed Painted Face.

But, the scene was an odd thing. With all the lakes and rivers alive with fish, these hunters would not think of eating them.

"Good Plains' hunter considered only buffalo, elk, moose, and deer fit for men and warriors. No fish! Never!" imparted Painted Face as one of his daily truths.

CHAPTER 31

Girl Free From Evil Spirits

"We go to the Country of Smokes!" said Painted Face.

Wandering here and there, the tribe got to know the rugged land as if they had lived there. They could find their way and estimate distances; they knew poisonous snakes from harmless ones; they read the weather from the shape of the clouds and time by the angle of her shadow; they knew what to do if they came across predators. They would never forget the bird-pecked corpse swinging from a tree and wearing a placard of warning. Tinkling Bell's people were frugal people; they lived on very little and required very little. They learned to live for the day and to appreciate all the wonders it had to offer.

To the northwest lay the Country of Smokes, better known today as Yellowstone Park. Painted Face regarded it with awe.

"See, giants breathe steam and hot water," pointed out Painted Face as they sprayed the skies.

There were places where mud bubbled forever in mighty cauldrons.

"It place of evil spirits!"

"Mountain of Black Ice too!"

Not only were the mountains believed to harbor evil spirits, but here could be found a mound of obsidian, which made the best arrow points and knives. Only a few men in the tribe had iron knives, but iron was too precious to be wasted on arrow points.

"I lead a party into the Country of Smokes for black ice," volunteered Painted Face.

"Take me, Father! Please take me!" pleaded Tinkling Bell to her father who only laughed.

"No girl child allowed near evil spirits," mocked Painted Face to his daughter.

Of course, no girl child could go on such a dangerous mission among evil spirits. But he liked to have his daughter at his side, so finally he gave in to her wish.

"I think your medicine is strong enough to bring you back safely," he said, "but just to be sure, we will have the chief medicine man make you a mighty charm to carry."

Painted Face paid two horses for the most powerful charm the medicine man could make, and in return Tinkling Bell was given the most powerful charm. They passed through a region where the three great peaks of the Teton Mountains in Wyoming towered against the sky. They left the sage brush country and entered a pine forest. They passed a long lake and a mighty river, which fell over a great cliff to roar down the deep, deep canyon of Yellowstone. They wandered to the top of high mountains.

"Look! Look, Father!" exulted Tinkling Bell, as she spread her arms outward over the entire country that lay below her.

Finally, they came to the Mountain of Black Ice. Here they gathered pieces of the volcanic glass and packed them carefully in leather sacks on the pack horses. They turned to go back, for no Native liked to stay long in this evil country.

"It's going to blow! It's going to blow!" sputtered Painted Face as the spouting holes began to…

gurgle

and

gurgle

and

bubble

and

bubble!

But, the geysers, those spouting holes where hot water was flung into the sky, did not frighten Tinkling Bell.

"Me not afraid! Me not afraid!" Tinkling Bell tried to convince her farther.

She was not frightened by anything. After all, she wore on her string of beads a charm against evil spirits for which her father had paid two horses to keep evil spirits from harming her.

So Tinkling Bell stayed behind in awe of the unfamiliar spectacle. Before her was a great plain smoking with steam. Amongst this fountain of hot water, steam, and mud there was nothing.

"I can't see my father or anyone else!" she wailed, as she rubbed her eyes to clear the moisture that had collected on them.

Steam from the many geysers had hidden the riders and their horses, and her own horse must have wandered away and been lost to sight in the same way. Her horse, too, was nowhere to be found.

"I will follow tracks of horses in mud," she whispered inwardly. "Surely my father will miss me?"

Hopefully, as the column moved forward her absence would be detected, and her father would circle back to where she was left.

But she followed the tracks for a whole day without sight of any living creatures. Tinkling Bell was not afraid of anything she had a wonderful time. She saw a canyon where rocks stood up like giants, and she reached a place where hot water poured over rocks to form terraces of pink and purple and bright red. At the time Tinkling Bell did not know that this would be named Mammoth Hot Springs someday.

"This earth warm," shared Tinkling Bell about the earth she slept upon that night. "No evil spirits visit me!" All hope had evaporated for Tinkling Bell.

Tinkling Bell slept below the whispering pines, and no evil spirits came to invade her dreams; neither did anything harm her. Wandering for five days in a white-hot rage, she was a volcano waiting to erupt.

"It is easier to save the soul if the body is healthy," she whispered to quiet her rage and fill the awkward silence. Then she took refuge in uncomfortable silence.

The night seemed eternal, but soon the rays of the sun back lighted the profile of a human. Early that morning she was awakened by a loud, scornful laugh. Her lack of horse sense left her unable to distinguish the guffaw that stirred her. There was her father, Painted Face, looking down at her quite pale from the top of his horse.

"Hurt?" he asked with a concerned look at Tinkling Bell.

"And where have you been all this time?" she questioned.

She was disturbed when she caught a glimpse of horror in his eye. Tinkling Bell was about to cross a threshold and leave her innocence behind.

Painted Face dismounted his horse. Tinkling Bell was impressed by his speed, precision, and strength. Sitting down beside her, he told a story that seemed like a fairy tale. However, it explained it all why she didn't see a living thing when she was screened by the geyser.

"You screened by smoking geyser," her father said. "Just at that moment a band of enemy warriors closed in on our party. There was no way to hold back the invaders. My companions and I drew them down a canyon and, after a battle in which three men of my party were wounded, they had beaten the other band and took many horses."

"With full war gear?" asked Tinkling Bell, stupefied at what she was hearing.

"The sad beings deprived of personality and robbed of spirit," accused Painted Face, fumbling in fury. Throughout the hideous exchange, a river of tears built in Tinkling Bell until they ran down her cheeks and bosom. Then she squeezed her hands together and stared into space, totally undone.

"We stung enemy warriors like wasps, exhausting their resources and patience."

Painted Face detested treachery of any kind and lived to protect others from harm.

"I am sick of so much horror and atrocities. There is nothing noble or glorious about war. There is nothing honorable in battle with enemy warriors when there are no rules. Rules count for nothing. The only standard is to win whatever the cost." Painted Face's heart was galloping and his brow was wet from perspiration.

Through systematic observation he learned to read character, and he applied his knowledge to protect Tinkling Bell. He could only imagine her with no defects. Through observation Painted Face learned about the duplicity of human beings. He read people's actions and discovered that words do not always correspond to intentions. He learned from the enemy warriors that the loudest are the least sincere, that arrogance is a quality of the ignorant, and the flatterers tend to be vicious.

"Geyser save my life," shared Tinkling Bell with her father gratefully.

Painted Face let out a maniacal howl that shook the walls of the canyon. Because of their mercurial naturesPainted Face ruled through courage and justice, unlike Tinkling Bell who was concerned with respect and dignity.

"Get on my horse behind me," requested her father, and together they found their band and wound through the mountains back to the big camp.

"What did you see?" asked all her friends when Tinkling Bell returned to the camp.

She was the envy of all her friends, for she had seen things unbelievable. The trip set her quite apart in the tribe, for she had led a charmed life in evil country. Because of her enchantment with adventure, her tribe changed her name. No longer was she to be called Tinkling Bell, but Girl-Free-From-Evil-Spirits.

CHAPTER 32

Familiar Shores

The workings of the dream catcher were pure *magic*! It had taken Nelson Paige far from familiar shores in time, space, and proportion that marked the beginnings of our country. There was no doubt in Nelson Paige's mind that his heart had been strengthened in his travels and his spirit empowered. He was leaving behind his friends, Buffalo Calf and Buffalo Hide in a time unlike his own, a time when travel was limited to animals, when space had no boundaries, and when proportions were out of necessity.

As a schoolboy, Nelson Paige was required to possess the basic knowledge of the geography of the United States. He could now give a general description of the "Great American Desert" where the Plains People made their home. The boundary of the Great Plains was now explicit to him: on the north bounded by the Upper Missouri, on the east by the Lower Missouri and Mississippi, on the south by what is now Texas, and on the west by the Rocky Mountains. With the boundary moved back by civilization to a distance of nearly three hundred miles west of the Missouri river, it came to be known as "The Plains." It is here where he came to know Buffalo Calf and the Plains People.

After two springs had gone, on a morning of white clouds and calm wind, Nelson Paige saw the images of the Plains People gradually diminish. The sun overhead was disappearing, and so too were the powers of the dream catcher waning. He continued to the very last moment to peer through the sinew of the dream catcher not to miss the story of Plains People written in sinewy style. Finally, their images were entirely blotted out, Elk-Woman and her sisters rescuing the braves from the turbulent waters of the flood.

All night he did not sleep, thinking of Buffalo Calf and Buffalo Hide as they called out to him during the disastrous flood.

Their voices echoed in his mind for a long time since the night of the flood. Every day he had gone to fetch the dream catcher and watched it closely, always at dusk and periodically at dawn. For it was through the catcher he learned of another culture, that of the Plains People.

Making himself comfortable in the confines of his comforter and wrapping his pillow about his head, he grasped the dream catcher for one more time. What made Nelson Paige special was his ability to dream a reality of the past; of course, the help of his dream catcher aided this. He now clenched the dream catcher purchased by his grandfather at The Treasure Trove more tightly than ever; after all, it helped him to travel and grow and learn and empower him.

Then he did something that made him smile. He held the dream catcher up to the window as to change his perspective. The effect of distance on space relationships was about to change. He must go to immediate life itself, which is always far from daring, than the effect of the imagination. Then the sounds came that made that change.

Ping! Ping! Ping!

Turning his head away from the dream catcher once again toward the intermittent, periodic pings on the surface of his window, he saw his friend, Judd Levin. Apparently, he had served his study hall detention with Mr. Coles and was on the move again. He couldn't wait to see if he made Mr. Coles scream like a baby. Pushing the dream catcher under his pillow for the last time Nelson leapt from his bed and ran down the stair steps, two at a time, until he reached the front door. There stood Judd. Ecstatic, they went outside, clapping each other on the back, not believing they were lucky enough to have each other as soul mates.

The morning was full of the glaring, gold light that poured out from the sun. The wind smelled of morning freshness and the things that lived in it. He shook his head and smiled at Judd Levin. He spoke again, slowly this time, and though his words sounded the same as before, he seemed more empathetic. It was the sound of a human voice, words that sounded like they came from a detention student. Judd Levin had changed like the front and backside of a picture. To Nelson Paige there was a definite attitude adjustment on Judd Levin's part.

"*I guess Mr. Coles made him cry like a baby,*" Nelson thought to himself for such a change to have taken place in his friend Judd Levin.

Nelson lifted his hand and gestured in the direction of Mt. Vernon Middle School. He made a picture in the air of what could be interpreted as it's time to move on. Judd Levin had a quiet smile of one who faced an obstacle and surmounted it with some degree of success.

Nelson Paige gestured a second time. To this Judd Levin nodded, and they were off to a new day at school.

*"Go confidently in the direction of your dreams.
Live the life you have imagined."*

Henry David Thoreau…

AUTHOR'S NOTE

In any case, dear reader, there I have related to you my story about Nelson Paige and his enchantment with the adventures of the Plains People. Nelson had made a long voyage with incomprehensible lightness to discover the voyage. If I might skip ahead a bit, you will find that Buffalo Calf has stirred up in Nelson Paige an appetite to learn all that he can about the Native American culture. I know you may feel what has been reported to you hangs an air of unreality. However, the life of the Plains People is true told through the magic of a dream catcher, a valued possession of the Plains People. Nelson has already been to the People of the Forest and Lakes (Iroquois) in *Nelson Paige and the Treasure Trove*. In *Nelson Paige and the Dream Catcher* he makes a long journey with the People of the Plains (Pawnee/Cherokee). Next, he will walk with incomprehensible lightness with the People of the Rivers and Sea (Okanogan) in *Nelson Paige Rides a Whale*. Finally, his travels will take him to the People of the Deserts and Mesas (Navajos) in *Nelson Paige and the Turquoise Sky*.

www.ingramcontent.com/pod-product-compliance
Lightning Source LLC
LaVergne TN
LVHW041947070526
838199LV00051BA/2928